A SCOT TO LOVE AND PROTECT

Once Upon a Scot Series
Book Three

by Maeve Greyson

Dragonblade Publishing, Inc. is an imprint of Kathryn Le Veque Novels, Inc.
P.O. Box 23
Moreno Valley, CA 92556
ceo@dragonbladepublishing.com

Produced in the United States of America

First Edition August 2022
Trade Paperback Edition

ARE YOU SIGNED UP FOR DRAGONBLADE'S BLOG?

You'll get the latest news and information on exclusive giveaways, exclusive excerpts, coming releases, sales, free books, cover reveals and more.

Check out our complete list of authors, too!

No spam, no junk. That's a promise!

Sign Up Here

www.dragonbladepublishing.com

Dearest Reader;

Thank you for your support of a small press. At Dragonblade Publishing, we strive to bring you the highest quality Historical Romance from some of the best authors in the business. Without your support, there is no 'us', so we sincerely hope you adore these stories and find some new favorite authors along the way.

Happy Reading!

CEO, Dragonblade Publishing

Additional Dragonblade books by Author Maeve Greyson

Once Upon a Scot Series
A Scot of Her Own (Book 1)
A Scot to Have and to Hold (Book 2)
A Scot To Love and Protect (Book 3)

Time to Love a Highlander Series
Loving Her Highland Thief
Taming Her Highland Legend
Winning Her Highland Warrior
Capturing Her Highland Keeper

Highland Heroes Series
The Guardian
The Warrior
The Judge
The Dreamer
The Bard
The Ghost
A Yuletide Yearning (Novella)
Love's Charity (Novella)

Dear Reader,

For this story, I chose Caerlaverock Castle in Dumfries, Scotland as the Maxwell stronghold under siege by the English in 1277.

Historically speaking, while this castle *was* the Maxwell family stronghold from the 13th century to the 17th century, it was more than likely built sometime between 1280 and 1300. The English *did* eventually seize it, but not until 1300. During that attack, the Maxwells fought valiantly and repelled the English many times, but in the end, they had no choice but to surrender. Imagine how the English army felt when they discovered that a mere sixty men inside that triangular castle had held them off so long. Quite a feat for the Maxwells and often celebrated in reenactments at the castle, which is now under the care of Historic Environment Scotland, a non-department public body of the Scottish Government.

For the sake of this romantic tale, you will see I have taken some fictional liberties with the castle's timeline, the Maxwells, and the lessons they learn. Please bear that in mind as you read it. And remember, all these characters are purely fictional and products of my imagination! Any resemblance to anyone living or dead is purely coincidental.

If you would like a peek at Caerlaverock (as well as hear the proper pronunciation), check out this YouTube video made by the tour guide of the castle: https://youtu.be/vTpVABe7yis.

Also, if you look it up on Google maps, then drop the little yellow man on the castle's location, you can "virtually" walk through it. I fell down that rabbit hole several times! It is so interesting to move through the actual courtyard and zoom in on every detail.

And if you are a member of the Maxwell clan, remember—no family is all good or all bad. People are just—people. I married a proud Maxwell descendent. One of the good ones. ;)

All my best to you,
Maeve

CHAPTER ONE

Caerlaverock Castle
Dumfries Scotland
July 1277

"THERE, CONSTABLE. JUST beyond that farthest line of cottages. I dinna believe the lights in those trees belong to the villagers."

Valan MacDougall agreed with William, his second in command, even though every dwelling in the small settlement looked deserted. Why would the inhabitants be out wandering in the forest at his hour? Several torch stands blazed here and there between the buildings. An eerie emptiness haunted the place. The craftsman and crofters of the clan appeared to have retreated to the safety of the castle. The Maxwells must have lit the stands to help them watch over the village from the safety of the fortress's battlements.

"The English are lax in their siege," Valan observed quietly. "They shouldha burnt Caerlaverock's village down afore now." From their position at the edge of the small, wooded rise to the west of the castle, he strained to see if his men had reached the back of the fortress. From there, wagons with stores to replenish the castle's supplies could safely cross the moat via the narrow bridge leading to the postern gate.

The rest of his men awaited orders on how he wished to dispose of the cowards attacking a castle defended by a pair of helpless women, their servants, and a handful of guards left behind when Laird Maxwell joined the battle in Wales.

A mizzling rain along with the densely wooded landscape bordering the clearing hindered Valan's view of his detachment's progress with the supplies. Handpicked from the Lord of Argyll's vast army of mercenaries, he knew his men would see the duty completed. But this was his first campaign as constable, leader of the massive, warring men descended from the long-ago mixing of Viking and Highlander blood. The mighty *Gallóglaigh*. He would not tolerate the smallest failure attached to his name. He gave the signal. "Let us extinguish the English's plans as well their torches, aye?"

Silent as spirits of the night, the warriors streamed down the hillock. They scattered into the village, melting into the shadows. The blazing torch stands throughout the village created ample enough places to hide.

All the while, Valan kept his gaze locked on the enemy's fiery brands trickling out from the trees. The flickering torches bobbed ever closer. Sword in one hand, double-sided axe in the other, he charged past the dovecote, then came up short when a familiar whizzing sound passed by his ear. Arrows from the rooftops? Clan Maxwell's archers must think them the feckin' enemy.

"Shields!" he bellowed.

His weaponry knave snatched the axe from his hand and thrust an iron-banded disk of oak in its place before Valan had time to draw another breath and shout the next order.

"Only the English die! Dinna harm any of Clan Maxwell." He spun and faced the dovecote, banging his sword against his shield. "We be the MacDougalls! Save yer arrows for the English."

Another arrow glanced off the iron rim of his shield and hit his helm with a metallic ping. A sweeping glance at the skirmish assured him his men were almost out of range of the Maxwell archers. The English's torches and their bearers would soon be extinguished without his aid. Shield held high, he stalked closer to the dovecote, determined to make that particular Maxwell understand. "Cease fire, I say! We come to fight at yer side. We are the Lord of Argyll's *Gallòglaigh*."

"Get down!" The woman's shrieked warning came too late. Her arrow lodged in his shoulder, its tip finding a weak point between his broad, metal chest plate and the seam of his chainmail sleeve.

"Hell's fire!" Valan ripped the missile free of his flesh and threw it to the ground. Thankfully, the thing had not gone deep because of the angle of its flight. He contemplated retrieving it for use as a switch to redden the careless woman's arse.

"Hold fast!" she called to him as she climbed down from her perch. "I am coming to help ye." Before he could respond, she paused in her descent and bellowed loud and clear, *"Marbhadh na Sasannaich a-mhàin. Tha na h-Albannaich sin caraid."*

Kill only the English. These Scots are a friend. Valan snorted as he watched the arrows from the rooftops shift their arc toward the few remaining English. At least now, the Maxwells understood them to be allies. He rolled his injured shoulder, glaring at the silhouette of the brazen lass headed his way. She appeared to be dressed in the armor of a man. The wound she had inflicted irritated him more than caused him any pain. She would do well to take herself elsewhere. He turned to join his men.

"I said *hold fast!*" She charged to him with a fury that reminded him of his brothers' wives and latched hold of his arm. When he planted his feet and refused to move, she muttered a stream of Gaelic curse words under her breath. "Come with me now," she said. "The others can finish the fight. Let us hie to the castle so I might mend the error of my arrow's hasty release."

"Hie to the castle yerself, woman. I fight with my men." He'd taken naught but two full strides when she grabbed hold of his arm again and yanked.

"The fight is won, sir. Set yer pride aside so yer eyes might see the truth of it." While the dancing shadows hid her features, there was no mistaking the righteous fire and indignation in the regal timbre of her voice.

She was right. The fight was won. But he'd be damned if he admitted it to her. If not for his strict order to his men to leave the women of Caerlaverock alone, he would seek her out later once things calmed. Such a fierce minx would guarantee a most pleasurable coupling. That would definitely mend the error of her arrow's hasty release. The lost opportunity made him regret giving that order.

"Hie yerself to the keep and see to yer mistress," he said, adopting a tone sure to shame the headstrong woman and remove her temptation from his presence.

Her soft, bubbling laugh possessed the duality of a double-edged blade. Not only did it stir his temper but awakened his cock as well.

"I amuse ye?" He rolled the haft of his sword in his palm, ready to lay the flat of it across the impudent maid's arse.

"Aye, ye do." With the grace and loftiness of a queen, she offered her hand. "Allow me to introduce m'self, sir. I am Lady Elspet Maxwell. Mistress of this keep."

"Lady Elspet?"

"Aye." Her mirth made the simple word sound like a song.

Valan clenched his teeth so tight his jaws ached. Thank the gods for the shadows of the flickering torchlight. He took her hand and bent over it but refused to surrender and touch his mouth to her skin. "Forgive me, Lady Elspet, but I feel sure ye understand my confusion."

"Confusion?"

Her tone remained entirely too amused for his liking. "Aye. The lady of the keep should be safely behind the walls. Not in harm's way. Running unguarded in the village."

"Do I not recall ye saying ye fought *with* yer men? Not from the safety of a perch?"

No snub came to him to counter her feckin' wit. "Aye."

With an infuriatingly graceful tip of her head, she turned and strode away. "I must see to my clan, sir." After a few steps, just as she came even with a torch stand, she turned back, revealing a smiling visage so beautiful, he swallowed hard. His cock became even harder. "Yer name, sir, since ye speak as the one in command?"

"Constable Valan MacDougall." Not to be outdone, he graced her with a regal bow of his head. "Here to ensure that Caerlaverock remains yers, m'lady."

Her smile faded as she accepted his oath with the merest nod. "A most heartfelt welcome to ye, Constable. Yer skills are definitely needed to see that remains so."

"We shall oust the English, m'lady. I swear it." The sudden shift in her taunting mood to that of sadness troubled him. Made him want to fight off her demons until they left her in peace.

"It is not only the English who wish to seize Caerlaverock." She tossed an irritated glance at their surroundings, then flipped a hand as though shooing the thought away. "But that is grist for another day's milling." She stood taller and resumed her fearless demeanor. "Beitris! Come here now!"

He turned to see who the lady called, figuring it to be her maid. As young and lovely as Lady Elspet was, it could not be the daughter rumored to fight at her side. Her child could not be more than a wee lassie and was probably tucked away in the castle's nursery.

The Lord of Argyll had to have been misinformed regarding the details of the Maxwell situation. The MacDougall had clearly stated Laird Maxwell's widow and grown daughter fought side by side to prevent Caerlaverock's seizure by the English. Suspicion coursed through Valan. The MacDougall had been known to play games—especially when his wife got involved. And since Lady Elspet was a close cousin to Lady Christiana, there could be more to this campaign than merely securing the Maxwell lands. He resettled his stance as a smallish lad clad in full armor and helm trotted toward them with a longbow in his hand.

The narrow-shouldered warrior held up three fingers. "Three, Mama. Clean kills all."

"English for certain?"

"Aye, Mama." The proud lass tapped the tip of her longbow against the toe of her black boot. "From the smithy's roof, I could tell by the fighting that these fine, braw Scots hadna been tainted by Edward to turn on us."

Even though the lass's elaborate visor and camail hid her face, Valan could tell she was smiling. Gleeful pride filled her voice.

"Then, well done indeed, my daughter." Lady Elspet waved her closer. "Remove yer helm so ye might properly greet Constable MacDougall, commander of the Lord of Argyll's *Gallòglaigh*."

With a graceful sweep of her hand, Beitris revealed herself. The lovely young woman was the light to her mother's dark. A tumbling mass of bright copper curls framed her face, creamy and pale as fine ivory. Her fair skin glowed in the torchlight. He looked from her to the Lady Elspet whose lustrous ebony mane enhanced the richness of her complexion that was warm and tempting as a lightly toasted bannock.

Lady Elspet smiled and linked her arm through her daughter's. "Beitris inherited her father's coloring. But she got my stubbornness—so take care."

Valan blinked to break his stare. Mother would have cuffed him for such rudeness. Manners recovered, he made an apologetic bow. "Forgive my boldness, but the two of ye seem more like sisters than mother and daughter."

Beitris snorted, then smiled up at her mother who stood a head taller. "Not original, but he does seem more honest than the others." She winked, then nudged Lady Elspet's shoulder with her own. "This one doesna have the nauseating guile of the old dogs Da used to send sniffing around me."

"Beitris."

Valan recognized Lady Elspet's scolding tone as the well-honed weaponry of a true mother. The lady must have borne her daughter at a shockingly young age. He offered Beitris another polite bow. "Constable Valan MacDougall at yer service, m'lady."

"Might I train with yer men, Constable? I have mastered the

bow, but my skills with the sword and spear are sadly lacking. I am in dire need of practice and instruction."

Before Valan could utter a resounding *nay*, Lady Elspet stepped between them. "To the castle with ye, Beitris." She pointed in that direction. "'Tis times like these that show me the error of my ways. Yer father and I indulged ye too much. Off wi' ye now. Find Fiona and hie yerself to bed." After an angry shake of her head, she continued, "Train with the mighty *Gallòglaigh*, indeed. Where is yer mind, girl?"

Beitris snapped her mouth shut into a tight-lined pout. Her cheeks flushed an angry red, and she stomped away.

"I trust ye willna heed her request, aye?" The lady ran a weary hand across her brow as she watched to ensure her daughter entered the gatehouse as instructed. "I had hoped by the age of ten and eight, she wouldha garnered more interest in womanly things, but I fear it shall never be. 'Twill be quite the chore finding a man able to cherish such a wife."

"States the mother who also dresses in armor and appears quite adept with a bow."

Lady Elspet turned a hard glare upon him. "My home is loyal to Scotland and King Alexander. Since my husband cared more for Wales than his land or his life, protecting Caerlaverock has become my responsibility."

Valan immediately regretted his comments—as he often did, since he possessed neither the desire nor the ability to keep his thoughts to himself. "Ye no longer fight alone, m'lady. A score of *Gallòglaigh* are now at yer disposal." It occurred to him that while she would appreciate their sword arms, she might consider keeping them fed and watered a burden. He hurried to reassure her. "And we have brought enough supplies to not only restock yer stores but provide for ourselves as well. We shall be a blessing. Not a burden, I assure ye."

Her scowl softened, but her tone did not. "We shall see, Constable." With a last glance at the now quiet village, she turned and headed toward the gatehouse with the determination and pace of a charging warhorse. "More will come at sunrise. I recommend ye warn yer men and divide them."

"Divide them?"

Her rapid pace halted. She turned and eyed him as though he had sprouted a set of horns. "The English attack both at night and during the day. Do yer men have no need of sleep?"

How dare she insinuate they were naught but a gaggle of fools who had no inkling of how to win a battle. "This is not our first campaign."

"I am glad to hear it." She resumed her long-legged stride toward the castle. "I shall await ye in my personal hall where I will see to yer wound. It must be properly cleaned and stitched to prevent festering. The servants will direct ye to my private floor. 'Tis the level above the garrison. Part of the gatehouse."

"My provisions knave shall see to me, m'lady." He didn't come here to be pampered by the mistress of the keep. Although, from what he had seen so far, under other circumstances, he would gladly welcome her attention.

She halted again, then backtracked until they stood toe to toe. Taller than most women he had met, she still had to look up at him, and he could tell she didn't like it. Good. Something about frustrating this intriguing woman pleased him to no end.

"Ye would insult yer host by refusing aid and hospitality?" Her tone rang with the regal authority of a queen holding court.

"Since it was my host who inflicted the wound, I dare say the insult is warranted."

"I apologized."

"Ye did not, m'lady." He motioned for his weaponry knave to come forward and take his shield and sword, then folded his arms across his chest. His chainmail clinked against the metal chest plate, gleefully ringing out the challenge of his stance. Even in the poor lighting he could tell her delicate nostrils flared. Well met. His challenge had been accepted.

Her hands closed into fists. "I bade ye to hold fast so I might render aid. I dare say that is apology enough since ye couldha been lying about who ye were. Ye would nay be the first group of Scots turned traitor for the Hammer's favor."

Edward I, known as the Hammer of the Scots because of his brutal tactics against Scotland, would resort to anything to win. Valan had encountered old Longshanks once. Faced him toe to toe just as he now stood with the lovely Lady Elspet. But before he could separate the man's head from his body, the bastard's men rushed in to defend him. By the time Valan sliced through them, Edward was gone.

"Well? What say ye?" She mimicked his challenging pose and jutted her chin upward. "I dare say ye wish to see to yer men afore ye accept the healing I offer. They may see to their rest and refreshment in the great banquet hall. Caerlaverock's mighty walls protect many right now, but there is room for yerself and all yer men." Her tempting mouth took on a wily slant. "The English will be quite surprised at the increase in our numbers in but one night."

Valan struggled with indecision. He sorely wished to either kiss her silent or have her locked in her chambers for her own protection while he sent the English running with their tails tucked. Or both. "Ye are a stubborn woman, Lady Elspet."

Her mischievous look increased his desire to kiss her. "Ye are not the first to describe me in such a manner, Constable Mac-Dougall."

"I will allow ye to see to this wee scratch on one condition, m'lady." While warring filled him with endless energy, jousting with words wore him down. Especially when his opponent was a woman as quick-witted as this one.

"And what might that condition be?" She relaxed her defensive stance as if sensing victory.

"Ye shall grant me a boon for firing on me twice after I clearly announced myself as an ally and not an enemy."

"I had already loosed the first arrow before ye told me who ye were."

"That was yer excuse for releasing the second arrow as well."

Perhaps this jousting with words wasn't so wearying after all. For the first time since they started this dance, he detected the sweet scent of her uncertainty. "Which is it, m'lady?"

"What is this boon ye request?" She cast a quick glance all around as if she feared being overheard. "Well? Name it. We waste precious time, Constable."

"Call me Valan."

"That is yer boon?" Even in the shadows, he caught the sleek line of one of her dark brows arching in disbelief.

"Nay, m'lady. Not entirely."

"I shall grant one boon. Ye dinna deserve two."

"There were two arrows, m'lady." He allowed himself a smile but withheld a victorious chuckle.

"Fine." She resettled her feet like a frustrated hen scratching for bugs. "Pray tell, what is this second boon, *Valan*?"

He liked the way she said his name. The richness of her voice stirred him, making him long to hear her say his name repeatedly during bed play. "I would have yer kiss, m'lady."

Both her brows rose this time. "A kiss?"

"Aye." He offered her another smile, this one more suggestive. "Once ye finish cleaning and stitching my wound, I would have yer kiss."

"Shame on ye, sir." But her expression held no scolding. In fact, her look reminded him of the slyness of a cat about to pounce. "I am widowed naught but a few months, and yet ye would request my kiss? What would my clan think of such behavior?"

"I dinna think ye give a rat's arse what yer clan thinks." Valan dared to smooth an escaped strand of her silky hair away from her face. "If ye did, I hardly think yerself and yer daughter would wear armor and defend yer lands with the fury and vigor of any man."

Her lips twitched, but the subtle glint in her eyes convinced him it was because she wished to hide her amusement rather than anger. With a flip of her heavy braid, she stepped aside and resumed her course toward the gatehouse. "I shall await ye in my hall, Valan. Dinna tarry too long."

"Never ye fear, m'lady. I willna keep ye waiting." He admired her form as she walked away, wishing the wind would settle enough to stop the torchlight's flickering and allow the light to better outline her every curve.

"No losses," William said from behind him. "Who is the armored lass?"

"Our hostess," Valan said. He faced William after the beguiling woman disappeared inside the castle's walls. "The Lady Elspet Maxwell."

"The way our liege spoke, I thought the laird's wife to be aged and helpless." William stepped to one side, squinting at the gatehouse as if willing the stones of the fortification to reveal the lady within. "What of the daughter?"

"Lovely as her mother and more interested in the skills of sword, bow, and lance than in stitchery and cooking." He clapped a hand on William's shoulder. "Bear in mind our Lord of Argyll answers to his wife, Lady Christiana, and Lady Elspet is her close cousin. While I know our forces are needed here, I believe there is more to this quest than we are aware." He squeezed William's shoulder again and shook it. "Mind yerself and mind the men. I fear the wrath of the Lady of Argyll more than I fear the MacDougall. For the sake of us all, we must remain watchful."

"I shall remind each of them of yer order to leave the women alone." William thumped his fist to his chest. "Where shall I have the tents set?"

"No tents." Valan pulled in a deep breath, then hissed it out between his teeth as he aimed a single nod at the triangular-shaped castle. "We shall stay within those walls. The great hall is to be ours. Lady Elspet assured me there is room." He scanned the dark woods and rolling landscape surrounding the clearing around the castle. "Our watches from the battlements shall rotate to keep the men fresh, as well as ease any cramped conditions inside the hall or the courtyard. Since I have seen no villagers other than those fighting from the rooftops here, I wager they're sheltering inside the castle as well."

"I believe we almost outnumber the remaining Maxwells," William said. "After Gordon sent the supply wagons inside, he joined our wee tussle with the English curs. He reported verra few in the castle. Their laird left less than needed to guard these lands. 'Tis a wonder it hasna fallen to the enemy afore now."

A testament to Lady Elspet's vigilance. Valan looked forward to knowing the beguiling woman better. Few intrigued him. But she did. "See that all are within the walls soon. I prefer to surprise the English when they attack during the day."

"Ye dinna think they'll suspect something when those who attacked tonight dinna return?"

Valan allowed himself a wicked smile as he strode toward the castle. "I dinna ken. But I look forward to confirming their suspicions come daybreak."

"M'lord!" Marcas, his provisions knave who cooked, cleaned, and offered herbal remedies better than any wise woman of the woods, stepped out of the shadows. "Will ye be housing with the men or in separate quarters?" His narrow face tightened. "I see fresh blood on yer mail. How bad is yer injury, m'lord?"

"'Tis naught but a scratch, and Lady Elspet insists on tending it since it was she who inflicted it."

Marcas halted. His eyes flared wide, pushing his bushy brows to his thinning hairline.

Valan laughed. Marcas guarded his position as the constable's provisions knave with the jealousy of a new mistress. "Ye can examine her handiwork once I return to the main hall. 'Tis there where we shall settle, aye? Tell Niall as well so he can see to my armor. 'Twill need a good oiling after all this rain."

Marcas relaxed somewhat, enough to give a respectful bob of his head before bending to pick up the small trunk of herbs and healing tools he trusted no one to carry other than himself. "I shall see to everything, m'lord. As I always do."

"I know ye will." Valan made his way through the rest of the small village before anything or anyone else detained him. He looked forward to seeing Lady Elspet again and wished for no further delays. As he entered the gatehouse, he noticed the advanced age of both guards and the weariness lining their gaunt faces. He also noticed the relief in their eyes. This pair looked ready to drop to their knees and give thanks. "How many hours have ye been at this post?" he asked the white-haired man on the right.

With a sad smile, the old warrior shook his head. "I dinna ken, m'lord, and it doesna matter. My laird assigned me to this post, and here I shall stay as long as I am able." He pointed at a maid waiting at the far end of the corridor that opened into the courtyard. "Lady Elspet said to watch for ye. That there's Dullis. Waitin' to lead ye to her apartments."

Valan decided to test the exhausted man's capabilities. "And how do ye ken I am the one Lady Elspet said to watch for? How do ye know I am nay a spy?"

The elder gave him a toothless grin, then winked at the other guard. "She said ye was braw enough to tote a pair of fat Highland bulls. One thrown over each shoulder." He nodded. "I reckon that be yerself."

"She also said ye had long hair brighter than the whitest moonlight. Not from age, mind ye, but Viking blood." The guard on the left forced his bent body to straighten and gave a curt nod. "We may be long in the tooth, m'lord, but we still be as sharp as well-honed blades."

The guard on the right jerked a thumb toward the fidgeting maid. "Best be on yer way, m'lord, or Dullis will have all our arses."

Valan strode to the end of the tunnel-like entrance and glanced around the triangular courtyard. The silent, stern-faced maid didn't say a word or greet him with any show of respect. She simply whirled about and headed for the timber forestair leading to the upper floors. He ignored her insolence, blaming it on the wearing nature of the long siege. No matter. Her rudeness gave him permission to take his time and assess the surroundings.

He noted the kitchens, stores, a stone wellhouse, and a stable that appeared to include a small smithy's forge. The buildings attached to the interior of the reddish-hued sandstone skirting walls created a compact township as complete as the outside village beyond the moat. A pair of towers flanked the impressive gatehouse housing the guard's barracks and portcullis room. It looked to have room enough for prison cells as well. The imposing structure at the head of the castle created a wallhead battlement at the top that would supply a commanding view of the lands. Two more towers rose at the south end of the courtyard. Even though the castle had but three sides, the gatehouse at its front enabled the fortress four towers.

"M'lord," Dullis called out from the landing in the first turn of the forestair. "Her ladyship waits."

"So, she does." Valan took the wooden steps two at a time, sending the older maid scurrying up the stairs in front of him.

The harried woman, glaring at him as if ready to snap his neck, set her narrow shoulder against the massive arched door and bounced it open. After patting her simple white fillet and veil back in place, Dullis adopted a strained smile that turned her soured, wrinkled expression into a nauseating grimace. "Lady Elspet, are ye certain ye dinna wish to wait 'til morning to receive visitors? Ye've slept nary a wink in days."

Still dressed in her armor, the lady turned from staring out the window and shooed away the maid's concerns with a flip of a hand. "Ye worry too much, Dullis. Seek yer bed. The hour grows late."

"And leave ye here? Unguarded? With him?" Dullis resettled her footing and shot him a fierce glower, making him bite his lip to keep from laughing.

He bowed and thumped a fist to his chest plate. "Rest assured, I would do nothing to cause yer lady harm. Do ye truly think my liege's wife would allow me near her cousin if I were a danger?"

Dullis's scowl didn't lessen. If anything, it grew fiercer. With a curt nod to her mistress, she motioned toward a small bronze dish suspended inside a wooden frame. A delicate metal hammer lay on the table in front of it. "Strike the bell when ye be ready to retire." Her eyes narrowed as her focus sidled back to him. "I shall await yer call in the next room, ye ken? I shall be just inside the door, mind ye."

"Thank ye, Dullis." Lady Elspet waved her away again and waited until the door firmly clicked shut before turning back to him. She had loosed her dark hair from its braid and brushed it until it shone. The long tresses tumbled across her shoulders, making Valan yearn to run his fingers through its silkiness. "If ye will seat yerself here on the bench, I shall help ye with yer armor and mail so I can examine yer wound."

"'Tis quite heavy, m'lady. What say ye we merely share a drink and a conversation? As I said earlier, 'tis naught but a scratch that isna worthy of yer time. My knaves can see to both my armor and my healing."

"But that would negate our agreement, good sir, and no longer warrant the payment of yer boon." The candlelight made her golden eyes dance like fine whisky swirling in a glass.

He had thought her beautiful in the dim light of the village torches. He had been sorely wrong. The lady was beyond breathtaking. There was not a power in Heaven or earth that would prevent him from collecting that boon. He seated himself on the bench and rested his hands on his knees. "I await ye, m'lady."

CHAPTER TWO

O F ALL THE things she needed right now, the distraction of this man was not one of them. Somehow, his presence and cocksure wit sharpened the talons of her loneliness. The loneliness and isolation that had plagued her for years.

Elspet shoved away the unsettled feeling and assumed a mantle of playfulness, shoring her defenses against all she read in Valan's eyes. She had resisted the temptation of taking lovers before. She would do so again. Beitris and her people came first. Their safety and happiness mattered most.

"Whisky, wine, or ale, sir?" She rested a hand on the whisky decanter, instinctively knowing that would be his choice.

One of his fair brows arched to a sly angle. "Sir?"

"Valan." She liked the feel of his name on her tongue. Somehow, it brought them closer. "Whisky?"

"Aye, m'lady." He shifted on the bench and leaned back against the long, heavy oak table at the center of the laird's personal hall. Her hall now. Where she and Beitris took most of their meals.

His lopsided smile deepened the dimple in his right cheek, making his fierce handsomeness even more enticing. Dangerous weaponry indeed. "We should toast tonight's victory," he said, interrupting her observation.

"We should at that." She poured a generous amount of Clan Maxwell's best *uisge beatha* into a pair of glasses. "We should celebrate every victory even though we have yet to win the war." She put the stopper back in the decanter, set it on a wooden tray with the glasses, and carried the refreshments to the table.

Tonight called for more than one wee dram. This siege had lasted far too long, wearing her nerves raw and draining her emotional strength. And now she also had to contend with a man so tempting the possibility of finding comfort in his embrace threatened to weaken her resolve. In a show of stubbornness, she seated herself beside him and lifted her glass. "*Slàinte mhath.*"

"*Do dheagh shlainte,*" he said, touching his glass to hers. He downed the drink with a quick toss and set the glass on the table. "Ye're far gone weary, m'lady. I see it in yer lovely eyes. Dinna fash yerself about me, aye? Truly." He leaned close enough to make her catch her breath. The rumble of his voice, with its sultry richness, quickened her heartbeat. He smiled and lowered his voice to a husky whisper. "We can settle the matter of the kiss at another time, ye ken?"

"Elspet," she corrected, forcing a lighthearted tone. She downed her drink and rose from the bench. "If I am to call ye Valan, then ye must call me Elspet. At least, in private." She could do this. Play this game so the exciting warrior god would understand she stood strong against his seductive arsenal. An arsenal she knew had probably conquered many a woman. She was no fool. "Lift yer arm so I might undo the fastenings of yer armor."

His lopsided grin returned along with a knowing glint in those eyes that mirrored the color of a pale blue horizon right before dawn. "Elspet," he murmured softly as he lifted his right arm. "How is it ye ken so much about armor?"

She lifted both hands and turned in a slow circle. "Have ye failed to notice my apparel, kind sir?"

"I assure ye, lass, I have noticed everything about ye." His tone said so much more than his words.

She tensed to prevent an excited shiver from escaping but failed miserably at controlling the heat simmering at her core.

17

"Turn a bit. I canna undo the laces with ye leaning as ye are."

He complied.

Teeth clenched, she silently cursed her fumbling as she struggled with the snug leather ties. The heat of him stroked the backs of her fingers even through the layers of chainmail and quilted gambeson. "They have ye cinched in here tighter than Herbert ever wore his plating."

"Yer husband?"

"Of course, my husband." Heaven grant her the power of composure. She hadn't meant to snap like a hound guarding a bone. With a forced calmness, she moved to his other side. "Now, this arm?"

Valan lifted his left arm, his intense stare burning into her like a blazing arrow. "I am sorry for yer loss, m'lady."

"Elspet. Remember?"

"Elspet," he repeated. This time more solemn, as if Herbert's ghost had stepped between them. "As I said, I am sorry for yer loss. I understand it was naught but six months past. I am sure it is a difficult adjustment—learning to lead the clan without him."

"I am used to it. I have done it for well over eighteen years now. Closer, in fact, to nineteen." Clenching her teeth, she cursed her foolish tongue. She should not have said that. With a hard yank, she jerked the last of the leather fastenings loose, grasped the armor, and hefted it off over his head. Frustration strengthened her. Enabled her to manage the plating with barely a strain. If only her inner turmoil could be handled so easily. "There now. Chest and back plate off. Remove yer belt and lean forward. Then I shall help ye remove the hauberk."

He snagged hold of her hand and held her in place, staring up at her with those infernal eyes that saw right into her soul. "What do ye mean?"

"Undo yer belt," she repeated, knowing good and well that was not what he meant. "We canna remove yer chainmail or yer gambeson until ye do so."

"Elspet." A gentle scolding warmed his tone, stirring an increased fluttering in her middle. "What do ye mean when ye say ye have led yer clan alone all those many years?"

"My husband thought it his duty to join every skirmish, crusade, or campaign that King Alexander ever dreamed necessary." She flinched at the bitterness pinching her reply. "Forgive me. I get shrewish when I am weary." She nodded toward his belt. "Undo it, aye? So, we can get to that shoulder of yers before daybreak."

Concern creased his brow. Even more flickered in his eyes. They reflected a knowing, a dangerous understanding that threatened to weaken her resolve against his charms. He undid his belt and tossed it aside without shifting his gaze from hers. "Why would a man leave such a rare, beautiful woman alone for so verra long?"

She grabbed hold of his hauberk by the thick shoulder seams and yanked him forward. "I am neither rare nor beautiful." She forced a laugh. "And at a score and ten, I am also neither so vain nor silly enough to believe in such flattery."

"Ye became a mother when ye were not more than ten and two?" He pulled free of her grasp, scowling his disbelief. "What man would marry off his daughter at such a tender age? In fact, the youngest age of consent allowed by the church?"

With a step back, she drew in a deep breath and squared her shoulders. Valan made it more than a little obvious. She would never get to his injury until she explained her past. She had no one to blame but herself for this impasse. 'Twas a just punishment for triggering this snare with her wagging tongue.

"My father arranged my marriage. Or sold me, actually. He cared not if marriage was part of the bargain. Herbert offered him more than any of the others." She paused, struggling to find the words to explain. "My mother died in childbirth. As an unwanted daughter born late in life after four grown sons, the only value I brought my father was what he might barter for me. Even though Laird Herbert Maxwell was verra old. Old enough to be my grandsire, in fact. He was a kind man. He saw my father's disregard for my welfare and knew if he failed to step in and save me, things would go verra badly indeed."

"But ye were a child," Valan argued. "A wee lassie of ten and two is naught but a child."

"Not according to the church. And as I said, my father cared not if marriage was part of the bargain." She paused, poured herself another whisky, and downed it. "Of course, since he held off until I reached the age of consent, it made him appear pious and moral." She ran her thumb along her glass's rim, remembering the many cruelties committed in secret by her sire. "My father was verra much about appearances." She banished the man from her thoughts, refusing to waste another moment of her life on his memory. "And as I said, Herbert Maxwell was a man of great kindness. Patient. Good-hearted." She filled Valan's glass before filling her's again. "My fate couldha been much worse."

Valan downed his drink, then placed the glass back on the table. "No child should have to endure what ye did, patient man or no'." He rose from the bench and paced the length of the room. With a hard glare at her, he halted his agitated walking. "Did Maxwell tire of ye after he robbed ye of yer innocence? Is that why he left ye alone so much?" He stabbed the air with his finger. "And dinna defend him by saying he gave ye shelter and food. He shouldha behaved as a trusted guardian until ye were old enough to choose to be his wife."

"Yer views are not those of most men." What a confusing warrior. She studied him as he paced, coming to realize his distress had more to do with himself than her. What ghosts haunted his past? Subtle suffering shadowed his handsome features and tensed his broad shoulders. This man was in pain. "Why do ye believe the way ye do about women?"

He shook his head. "Nay, woman. Ye didna answer my question. Why did the bastard abandon ye?"

"Herbert was not a bastard. In time, even though I saw him little, he became a friend." Rather than look Valan in the eyes, she unlaced the long protective cuffs of heavy leather protecting her forearms. "A few months into our marriage, he was injured during a hunt." She tossed first one sleeve and then the other onto the table. "After he recovered, he found he could no longer..." A heavy sigh escaped her. She had never attempted to explain the reason for her lonely marriage before. "His manhood failed him. We could no longer...join."

Valan stopped pacing, but his disapproving scowl remained. "Why did ye not have the marriage annulled?"

She laughed. "And go where? My brothers and their wives had no use for me. They shared my father's low opinion of my usefulness." With a slow shake of her head, her laugh turned bitter. "And thankfully, Herbert had already fathered Beitris. His only child was growing within me when the accident robbed him of being a man." She filled both their glasses and held his out to him. "After that, his pride forced him to join every battle he could find. Said it was the only way he felt whole again." When Valan refused to take the drink, she added, "Tell me ye would not have done the same."

Still glaring like an ox about to charge, he strode forward, took the drink, and emptied it in a single gulp. Without a word, he yanked off his chainmail, then unbuttoned his gambeson, and tossed it aside.

Her mouth went dry at the hard, muscular glory of him. Even in his prime, her husband would never have come close to the sculpted majesty of this man. Over the years, she had often helped with healing and caring for the wounded. The task not only kept her busy but also helped her clan. Never had she seen a man made like this one. She pointed at the bench. Sheer, stubborn willfulness enabled her to maintain a calm exterior. He must never know the powerful effect he wielded. "Sit so I may clean yer wound. I canna reach it as well when ye stand."

He lowered himself to the bench, sitting in silence with his head bowed.

She hurried to the cabinet at the back of the room and gathered all she needed to clean, stitch, and bandage a wound caused by an arrow.

"Did ye never think to take a lover?" he asked so softly she almost didn't hear.

She started to tell him it was none of his affair but stopped herself. Nay. This was the first time she had ever spoken to anyone about the aloneness she had borne over the years. It helped to tell her story. Her chest didn't feel quite so tight anymore, nor her heart so heavy. "Herbert gave me his blessing to take a lover. All he requested was that I be discreet." As she placed the bowl, linens, and bandages on the table, she frowned down at them, struggling with the memory. "I could nay do that to him. Not after he had been so patient and gentle with me." She released a heavy sigh and lifted her head. "I was fond of Herbert and would see no more shame thrust upon him. He was the first kind man I had ever known. With his pride already in tatters, I refused to add to his burden."

Valan locked eyes with her. "As I said, Elspet, ye are a rare and beautiful woman."

"Nay." She went to the hearth and fetched the iron kettle she had hung on the rod over the fire. "I am just a woman trying to live out my life in honor and dignity." With her hand wrapped in a rag, she lifted the steaming kettle and carried it back to the table. After adding hot water to the bowl, she mixed a generous amount of whisky in it before wetting a roll of linen in its steaming depths.

"I am sorry I shot ye," she said, now regretting she had shared her story. At first, it had brought her relief. But not now. Why in Heaven's name had she done so? What power did this man possess to pull such an outpouring from her? "Forgive me, aye?"

He didn't answer. Just leaned forward and propped his forearms on his knees.

"So ye dinna accept my apology?" she teased, trying to relieve the tension between them. The air throbbed with it. And she had no one to blame but herself. "Valan?"

"'Tis naught but a wee scratch," he said, but his heart wasn't in the denial. "Ye are quite forgiven, m'lady."

She repressed a weary sigh. So, it was to be that way between them? Well then, perhaps, it was for the better. She wrung out the cloth and daubed the dried blood from his skin, cleaning the area as gently as she could. A sad smile tugged at her lips as she managed the chore. Valan's claim that it was naught but a scratch had not been one of gallantry. He knew his injuries. The arrow tip had barely punctured his flesh and would only take a stitch or two to close, if that. "Ye were right about the wound, good sir. Perhaps I should practice more with Beitris to improve my archery skills."

He caught hold of her hand and halted her, fixing her with such a fierce gaze she forgot to breathe. "Nay, m'lady. Ye should keep yerself safe within these walls. My men and I shall handle the warring."

The muscles in his strong jaw flexed, entrancing her until she felt compelled to touch his cheek. He covered her hand with his and locked his eyes with hers.

"Yer boon, sir," she whispered, unable to help herself. The demons of her loneliness pushed her to touch her mouth to his, and all control left her. How could such a battle-hardened man possess lips so tender and sweet? The taste of whisky and exhilaration filled her as she deepened the kiss.

His arms encircled her, gathering her to the hardness of his chest. She stood between his knees, his muscular thighs flanking her, holding her just as tightly as his arms. He took control of their joining. The flick of his tongue to hers unleashed more of her demons, making her hunger for more.

"M'lady?" Dullis's high-pitched shout from behind the closed door shattered the spell. "M'lady, are ye ready to retire yet? Ye must get some rest, ye ken? I am ready to help undo yer armor."

With her fingers tangled in his hair, Elspet forced herself to break their connection. A disappointed gasp left her as she tore her mouth from his. "Forgive me," she whispered. "I forget myself." She pushed away and stumbled back, moving out from the intimate space between his knees. Before he could respond, she called out to the maid, "I am nearly finished, Dullis. Seek yer bed. I can manage my armor. I know ye rose well before dawn to help with the baking."

"Are ye certain, m'lady?"

Elspet closed her eyes in a futile attempt at calming the dangerous storm within. At the very least, she had to keep the raging turmoil out of her voice. Dullis had been with her quite a while. But of late, ever since Herbert's death, the maid's attitude toward her had changed. She had become almost defiant. "I am certain, Dullis. I have nearly finished dressing Constable MacDougall's wound so he can return to his men in the hall." She forced her eyes open but avoided Valan's gaze and busied herself with threading the needle for his stitches. She couldn't trust herself to look him in the eyes after that kiss. "Sleep well, Dullis," she called out with a glance at the door that was thankfully still shut.

"Sleep well, m'lady. Call out if ye have need of me."

Elspet bowed her head and waited, counting the maid's clunking footsteps against the wooden floors as they faded away. After a deep breath, she managed a smile while still keeping her attention locked on Valan's shoulder. "I think two stitches will do nicely. Possibly even one if I angle it just so."

"Ye canna pretend that kiss didna happen, m'lady." The mighty warrior sounded as distraught as she felt.

"Aye, dear sir, I can." He had no idea how good she was at pretending. She had done it all her life. 'Twas a matter of survival. "Hold still now. 'Twill sting a bit."

He snorted out a noisy exhale. "Elspet…"

"Yer boon is paid," she said softly, then tied off the needless stitch and cut it free with her small shears. "Shall I bandage it or do ye prefer yer knave to do so?" From the looks of the pale, thin lines scarring his chest and arms, his provisions knave appeared quite adept at caring for him.

He caught hold of her hands and pulled, gently forcing her to sit beside him. "I canna pretend that kiss didna happen." His calloused fingers touched the edge of her jaw, then slid into her hairline as he cupped her cheek. His eyes narrowed the slightest bit as his lopsided smile returned. "I commanded my men to leave the women of Clan Maxwell untouched, and yet here I sit, in violation of my own order." He leaned closer, his voice dropping to a rasping whisper. "And I would violate it as many times as ye can count, if ye would but permit it."

"I cannot." The scars across his muscular expanse of chest anchored her emotions in the oddest way. The reminder of his past battles gave her the strength to refuse him. This man lived by the sword. A mercenary. While his time in her bed would undoubtedly be bliss, once the siege ended, her solitary existence would return with a vengeance when he left her. Even in her desperation, her pride remained intact. To revel in his heated embrace in place of her cold bed would only make the loneliness worse when it came time for him to leave. She wanted more than fleeting pleasure.

"It took me many years to temper my yearnings and adapt to a life alone. I willna put myself through that again." She rose from the bench and put more space between them. The heat of him, his manly scent, muddled her thoughts, making it difficult to express herself so he might understand. "I willna be a prisoner to my loneliness and lower myself to becoming a passing distraction. Once the English retreat, ye will return to yer Lord of Argyll, and I will remain here. Caring for my people and securing a suitable husband for my daughter." She carried the basin of water to a bucket in the corner and emptied it. "Perhaps someday Fate will be kind enough to send someone willing and able to stay at my side."

He slowly rose from the bench and faced her. A pained expression creased his brow. "Ye know I want ye. Hell's fire, woman, I want ye more than I have ever wanted any woman. But I canna promise to give ye what ye seek because I willna dishonor ye with a lie."

She closed the distance between them and rested her hand on

the center of his chest. She needed the warmth of his flesh against hers, even though nothing more could pass between them. "I thank ye for yer honesty." The thud of his heartbeat into her touch made her smile. "Ye are a good man, Valan."

"Nay. I am not." He touched her face with a gentleness that made her aching loneliness keen for relief. "I dinna ken which will be the greater demon I must choose between—beating the English back with great haste so I might escape this temptation, or fighting the bastards at half strength so I can tarry here all the longer in the hopes of changing yer mind about us."

"Temporary pleasure can only bring regret." She spoke more to herself than him. The longer he stayed so close, the more her resolve weakened.

"Or give us precious memories to brighten a cold, bleak day?" He drew her closer still. "If I have learned anything about this life, it is that nothing is guaranteed. Not tomorrow. Not years from now. Not even the next hour. All we have for certain is the moment at hand. Nothing more."

She wavered, recognizing the truth of opportunities lost, never to be regained. "My cousin, Lady Christiana…" She forgot what she intended to say as he brushed the backs of his fingers along her cheek, then stroked her bottom lip with the calloused edge of his thumb.

"The Lady Christiana?" he encouraged while teasing a tender kiss to her temple.

She closed her eyes, holding tight to his forearms to keep from swaying off balance. This battle between her conscience, her pride, and her ravenous need was the fiercest she had ever fought. "Lady Christiana hated she couldna come to my aid all those years ago. But my marriage came to pass before she received word."

"She has come to yer aid now," he whispered against her hair. He slid his hands down her back and pulled her close enough to feel the hard length of him even through the leather panels of her armor. "She sent me."

What harm could come from a single night? Her need's whisper echoed in her mind with such force, she swore she heard the words out loud.

"One night." She almost choked on the words. "Just the one, ye ken?"

"Just the one, m'lady." His kisses burned a trail along her neck and behind her ear, sealing the promise like a searing brand. He scooped her up into his arms and cradled her like a babe. "That doorway?" He turned toward the arched portal, the one painted a deep red because that was her favorite color.

"Aye, but take care." She tucked her face into the curve of his throat, her courage and the rightness of this brave decision making her heart pound until it rendered her breathless. "Dullis's room is to the right as soon as ye enter." She lifted her head and gave him a warning look. "She said she chose it to better guard me."

"Then we must take care not to disturb her." The subdued rumbling of his quiet amusement tickled against her. "I am sure yer Dullis is verra fierce."

"She is indeed."

With every step closer to her bedchamber, her heart beat faster until she thought she would surely swoon. It had been so very long, and she was no longer a shy, bumbling young lass. She was a woman and knew what she needed. "There. That door is mine."

He crossed the cozy expanse of her small solar in naught but three strides, shouldered open the door, and stepped inside. Just past the threshold he eased her down to her feet and took hold of both her hands. "Ye are certain of this, m'lady?"

"Elspet," she gently corrected. "And yes. I am certain. One night." Nervousness tickled the corners of her mouth upward into a weak smile. "One night is to be my boon, ye ken?"

"So be it." He closed the door and lowered the wooden bar across it. With a glance back at her, he gave a slow, reassuring wink. "To protect me from Dullis, aye?"

She didn't answer. Instead, went to the hearth, stirred the banked coals, and added a stick of wood. More for light than warmth, since the lone candle flickering on the mantel did little else than mark the hours. The notched wax above the nail waiting to melt free and hit the metal plate on the hour before sunrise reassured her that a generous span of time was left to be enjoyed.

"I have naught but wine here in my room. Would ye care for a glass?" She gripped the edge of the small sideboard beside the bed. A churning mix of nervousness, yearning, and anticipation toyed with her balance. "I wish I had thought to bring the whisky," she added, cursing her mindless blethering. She stared at the lone glass beside the bottle of wine. There wasn't even a second glass. What could she do? Another trip past Dullis's doorway risked waking the slumbering beast.

"I need ye, Elspet. Nothing more."

She sensed him behind her, standing so close she tingled with the wanting of his touch. With a slow turn, she faced him and slid her hands up his hard ridges of muscle. "Such a broad chest," she whispered, not meaning to say the words aloud. A nervous gasp escaped her as she looked up at him, needing to explain. "It has been a verra long time since…" The ability to speak left her.

With a tender, leisurely caress, he combed her hair back from her face, then allowed the heavy tresses to slide through his fingers. "We will take our time with the ancient dance." He kissed her forehead, then her mouth, then brushed a whisper across her lips. "We will savor every sensation, every touch, every pleasure."

"Aye," she agreed with a hitching breath. Trapped within his gaze, she tugged free the strapping that kept the thick casing of her leather armor in place.

"Allow me to help." He lifted it over her head, leaving her in nothing but her linen tunic and the snug protective leggings she had reinforced with leather patching.

Before she lost her nerve, she untied the flap of her trews and slipped them off, leaving her in nothing but her liéne. The sudden memory of the faded, shimmering scars that rippled on either side of her taut belly made her hesitate. What if he had never been with a woman who had borne a child? Would the marks repulse him?

She bunched the hem of her shirt in her hands and ripped it off over her head. "My body isna perfect, ye ken?" She swallowed hard and lifted her chin. "But I proudly bear the scars of mother-hood."

His expression unreadable, he dropped to his knees, took hold of her buttocks, and pulled her close enough to flick the tip of his tongue across her stomach. "As I said before—twice even," he murmured between nibbling kisses. "Ye are a rare and beautiful woman, Elspet."

Unable to respond as he inched the heated trail of his tasting lower, she buried her hands in his hair and held on tight to keep from collapsing. Never had she imagined such sensations. When he slid his fingers up her inner thigh and then teased them across the slippery wetness of her opening, her knees buckled.

Somehow, he swept her up before she hit the floor and laid her across the bed. Either that or she floated on the pure bliss crashing through her body. The delicious waves hit harder as he lowered his mouth and sucked on her most sensitive part while churning his fingers inside her. She cried out, knotting the bedclothes in both fists, bucking beneath his ministrations.

"Shh...lass." He rose and swallowed her moans with a kiss. "Dullis will break down yer door," he whispered.

"I dinna care," she gasped, clamping her thighs around his narrow hips. "More, my fine warrior. Make haste and rid yerself of those trews. Yer expertise has made me greedy for more."

He flashed a smile down at her, his teeth a brilliant white even in the dimly lit room. Then he did as she bade and slid in deep and hard, pounding with a rhythm that made her arch and meet him thrust for thrust. Never had she enjoyed such mindless ecstasy. They moved faster, hotter, wetter. The delicious union melded them into one.

His deep, rumbling growl vibrated between them, starting low as if rooted in his belly rather than his throat. Elspet arched and threw back her head, calling out, "Valan!" again and again as wondrous spasms took control.

Arms locked, Valan plunged in and held fast. A roaring groan escaped him, tensing him hard as stone. A shaking overtook him until the joints of the bed rattled. Then he collapsed. "Forgive me," he gasped, struggling to roll to one side.

"Nay!" She pulled him back, hugging him close with her arms and legs. "The weight of ye warms me. Warmer than this cold bed has ever been." His hot flesh felt a part of her when pressed this close. She missed the feel of him as soon as he shifted away.

He settled back down and apologized with long tender kisses. Then he lifted his head and playfully touched the tip of his nose to hers. "Next time will be longer. Yer bed will nay grow cold this night. We are just getting started."

CHAPTER THREE

"**S**TAY AND SLEEP." Valan tried to pull her back into his arms, but she slipped free. "Elspet—ye closed yer eyes less than a moment ago."

"'Tis but an hour before dawn." Silhouetted by the soft glow of the dwindling hearth fire and the night candle burning low, she hurriedly donned her trews and cinched them at the waist. "The alarm nail melted free and hit the plate moments ago. I must prepare for whatever the day holds." She yanked her tunic over her head and shook it down in place. After a kiss that ended much too soon, she pulled free of him again and returned to gathering her scattered garments. "Our night is at an end, my fine warrior. Our boons are paid."

The boons between them would never be paid. He drew in a deep breath, filling his nostrils with the sultry scent of their loving still clinging to the bedclothes. God's teeth. He needed her all over again. Nay, their boons were far from settled. But Valan knew better than to argue the point at the moment. One night of passion with this remarkable woman only made him want her more. He pushed himself out of the bed and pulled on his trews. "I feel ye should rest. My men and I will handle whatever comes. See to yerself, Elspet. Ye no longer bear this burden alone."

She ignored him, pulling on her leather armor as if he hadn't spoken.

He caught hold of her arm and forced her to stop dressing

long enough to look him in the eyes. "Elspet. Listen to me—please."

"My people are as weary as I am. Some even more so. I willna insult them by claiming respite for myself when there is none for them." She rested a tender touch to his cheek, softening the refusal. "By the day's light, ye will see where the English destroyed almost half the settlement a mere fortnight ago. I canna lose the rest of castletoun under any circumstances. With every building that turns to ash, the hope in my clan's eyes diminishes." Her voice trembled with worry and frustration. "'Tis as if they toy with us. Attacking here and there, never fully razing even though they could. I dinna ken how to battle such tactics."

"M'lady?" Dullis rattled the latch and bounced the door against the bar. "M'lady! Be ye well?"

"I am better than I've been in a verra long while." Elspet gave Valan a wicked smile that hardened him even more. "Dinna fash yerself, Dullis. Hie to the kitchens for Beitris's morning meal. I can tend to my dressing alone."

"Will the Constable nay be needing the rest of his clothing, m'lady?" Dullis's sharp, disapproving tone left no doubt about her thoughts.

Her golden eyes dancing, Elspet playfully covered her mouth and then gave a shrug as she let her hand fall away. "The woman misses nothing," she whispered.

"Verra true, m'lady," Dullis grumbled through the closed door. "Got good hearing for one so aged, too." She rattled the latch again. "I have the Constable's clothes right here. If ye will open the door and take them, I shall fetch parritch and bannocks for him along with the morning meal for yerself and the Lady Beitris." Her fussing took on a warning tone. "And ye need to speak to yer daughter at first chance, yer ladyship. I saw her walking with one of those men that arrived last night. Got her hair all loose still and instead of a proper kirtle, she's wearing that armor again."

"I shall address that." Valan crossed the room, set the bar

aside, and yanked the door open. "I want the man ye saw with the Lady Beitris summoned to this hall immediately, ye ken?" Even though he ignored his own orders, he would not tolerate such behavior from his men. Besides, it was different between Elspet and himself. What they shared last night was a far cry from a light-hearted bedding.

The maid didn't move. Just glared up at him.

"Fetch him," he said, speaking louder. Insolent woman. How did Elspet tolerate her?

Dullis resettled her stance and glared up at him. Her determination to stand her ground unfazed by his stern tone. "Yer garments, m'lord." With a haughty sniff, she shoved them into his arms. "I shall fetch yer man before I gather this morning's repast." Her soured expression tightened further as she leaned to one side and peered around him. "Be ye well, m'lady? For true?"

Elspet came forward and stood at his side, as if ready to defend him. "As I said, much better than I've been in a long while, Dullis. This was my choice, ye ken?"

Relief and no small amount of pride filled Valan. Not only had he done right by his lady, but it seemed Elspet bore no regrets.

The elderly maid's perpetual scowl puckered even more. "Verra well, m'lady. I was but concerned for yer safety." Her fierce glare shifted to Valan as she continued, "I know about them *Gallòglaigh*, and I may be old but I am nay afraid."

The woman's loyalty made up for her insolence. Valan admired it and had no doubt she would either poison him or stab him in his sleep should he make the mistake of harming Lady Elspet. He pressed a hand over his heart. "I swear I willna hurt yer mistress."

"Oaths are as easy to break as they are to make." Dullis swung about and headed for the door leading to the stair.

"Dullis!" Elspet overtook the surly maid and barred her way. "Ye will treat Constable MacDougall and his men with respect until they prove they dinna deserve it. They came to help us and are honored guests. I will tolerate no more rudeness toward them. Is that understood?"

With a sullen jerk of her chin, Dullis stared down at the floor. "Aye, m'lady." She stole a glance at her mistress, then nodded. "Ye should cover yer hair with so many strange men about. Shall I bring a fillet and veil along with the food?"

Valan turned aside to don his remaining garments while the women discussed proprieties. He hoped Elspet wouldn't cover her lustrous hair. He longed to run his fingers through its silkiness again, remembering how it fell across his body in an ebony waterfall. With a stifled groan, he adjusted the seam of his trews to grant his hardened cock more room.

"She will be more respectful." Elspet picked up his long leather belt where he had laid it on the table. "And she has never been one to gossip." After a pensive look back toward the stairwell, she added, "That I know of, anyway. Of course, never have I given her such fodder before."

He took the belt out of her hands, tossed it to the table, and gathered her into his arms. "Whether she gossips or not, I regret nothing, and after all yer years of sacrifice to this clan, neither should ye question yerself, m'lady. Not about anything." A protectiveness swelled in his chest. A dangerous protectiveness he had seen his brothers display toward their wives.

"And what is this?" Lady Beitris stood in the open doorway, a brow cocked to a mischievous slant.

Valan stifled a smile as Elspet changed before his eyes. Gone was his ravenous lover. In her place, stood a mother goddess ready to unleash her fury upon her disobedient young.

Shoulders squared and hands fisted, she strode toward her daughter. "Did I not refuse yer request to train with the *Gallòglaigh*?"

Beitris puffed up, mimicking her mother's defensive pose. "Aye, Mama, and ye should know better than to accuse me of going against yer wishes. Have I ever done so?" With a remorseful shrug, she added, "Well...at least not over anything important?"

Not entirely certain he was doing the right thing, Valan stepped between the two women who reminded him of a pair of sparring Highland cats he had come across during a hunt. "Dullis reported seeing ye with one of my men," he explained, forcing a gentler tone than he would use on the man who had ignored his order.

"Dullis is a gossipy, meddling old cow who still thinks me a child." Beitris gave an impatient toss of her auburn curls. "And if she tries to cover my hair one more time, I'll be throwing her in the moat."

Before he could prevent it, a snorting laugh escaped him. "I shall help ye foist her high enough to get a good arc going over the wall."

"Valan!" Elspet's eyes flared wide, but then her kissable mouth trembled, betraying she wanted to laugh, too. She cleared her throat and assumed a regal stance. "Dullis is loyal and true," she said, her tone strained but controlled. "She is merely gruff. I feel certain, in her heart, she means well."

All amusement left Valan as a very unsettled William entered the hall with Dullis close behind, toting her broom like a weapon.

"This here's the one, m'lord. Saw him with me own eyes." The maid upended the broom and stamped its handle on the floor. "Walked entirely too close to the Lady Beitris earlier, and it not even sunup."

"I was walking the battlements," Beitris said. She took a step toward the old woman and gave another flip of her wild curls. "I always walk the battlements before we break our fast. 'Tis my turn. Mama walks afterward. Ye know that."

"What say ye, William?" Valan noted the young man's hesitancy to look him in the eyes.

After stealing a glance at Beitris, William stood taller. "I felt the lady shouldna walk alone. What if an attack broke out?"

"Inside the castle?" Valan stared at his second in command. If the man was going to lie, he should at least try to make it convincing.

"Beitris?" Elspet lowered a disapproving glare on her daughter.

The wily lass rolled her eyes. "Saint's bones, leave the poor man be. 'Tis my fault. I admit it."

"I am not a poor man," William said, sounding more insulted than he should.

"Aye, ye are, and ye're loyal to the marrow of yer bones as well." Beitris huffed an unladylike snort of disgust. She turned to Valan and held up a single finger. "Not only did he refuse to show me one move, just one mind ye, that might improve my swordsmanship, but he also said he would send word to my mother if I got anywhere near yer men."

"Well done, William." But Valan sensed there was more to this story. Even a blind man could see the fidgeting young warrior couldn't keep his besotted gaze off of the fiery Lady Beitris. He sympathized with his second in command. Lady Elspet possessed the same power over him. Must be some ancient magic the Maxwell women shared. He gave a dismissive nod. "Ye may go, William."

"Can he not break his fast with us?" Lady Beitris snagged hold of William's arm as he passed her. She aimed a coaxing smile at her mother. "After all, I did trick him."

"Ye did not," William argued.

"Aye, I did." Beitris adopted a coy tip of her head. "Can he, Mama? Please?"

Elspet sighed and drew a hand across her brow. After a glance at Valan, she gave a curt nod. "Aye. He can." She turned to Dullis. "Have Caitra and Fiona help ye with the additional trays. Or one of the kitchen lads. Whichever ye choose."

Dullis thumped her broom handle again, then departed, muttering under her breath.

"Ye are a dead man now," Valan warned William.

"Ye mean to kill me?"

"Not I." He grinned at the nervous warrior, then glanced at

the door the maid had left ajar. "That old woman."

"Dinna fash yerself, sir," Elspet assured William. "I feel sure she intends to kill the constable here first."

"And why is that Mama?" With a wicked grin, Beitris seated herself at the end of the table.

"Beitris." Elspet uttered the one word only, but even Valan noticed an immediate chill in the air.

Beitris bowed her head, then went to her mother's side, and knelt beside her chair. "Forgive me, Mama. Ye ken how I forget myself. Especially with…"

"That is enough." Elspet shooed her back to her seat. After a long, tense moment of silence, she pushed herself up and strode to a narrow door in the far corner of the room. Hand on the latch and head bowed, she spoke without turning around. "I have lost my appetite." Then she turned and met eyes with Beitris. "See that our guests eat their fill, aye?" She offered an apologetic smile to Valan. "The battlements call me. Should ye have need of anything more this morning, Beitris or Dullis will see it done."

Before he could respond, she left and closed the door firmly behind her. Valan stared at the portal, trying to decide whether to give chase and discover the reason for his lady's escape or grant her the solitude she seemed to need. A persistent tapping on the table pulled him from the quandary.

"She acts like that because the evil one is coming." Beitris leaned forward and glanced around as if the walls might overhear and betray her.

"Evil one?" Valan eyed the young lass, hoping she was as loose-lipped as she had accused the elderly Dullis of being. The bench beneath him creaked as he leaned forward and propped his forearms on the table. "Explain, lass. For yer mother's sake, so I might help her. Is it an Englishman ye speak of?"

Beitris hopped up from her chair and rushed to light on the bench directly opposite him. After a worried look at the door, she climbed up and knelt on the bench, then stretched across the table and lowered her voice to a whisper. "He is nay English. In fact, Dullis is on his side because he is a Maxwell, so dinna speak of him around that cow, aye? 'Tis the only one of Da's brothers still living. Euban is his name. Been after Mama for years. Even before Da died, he tried to seduce her." She shuddered as a look of revulsion curled her mouth. "He even cornered me in the well house once, but Mama sliced off his ear with her favorite dagger. Had him ousted from Caerlaverock after that. But that was before we got word that Da had fallen in Wales. Now, the worm is headed back here. Sent a messenger to one of Da's old advisors. That old goat's always disliked Mama and wanted Euban as laird."

A red haze of pure rage filled Valan's vision. Each of his knuckles popped one by one as he tightened his hands into fists. "I will gladly kill both the bastards and relieve yer mother of their existence."

Beitris patted the table and shook her head, her eyes flaring wide with alarm. "Nay. Mama fears if anything ill happens to Euban or Granger either one, especially here at the castle, the entire clan will turn on her. Many support Euban taking Da's place as laird since Mama is neither a full-blooded Scot nor landed in her own rights. She brought nothing when she came to Clan Maxwell. Cost them money, in fact, and they resent her for it. They think her a liability that will only cost them more. Especially if she ever remarries."

"Is this clan so feckin' ungrateful?" Valan rose, unable to sit any longer. "Yer mother dedicated her life to those people." He jabbed the air, pointing at the lass. "And ye both risk yer lives to save their village and them."

"'Tis not the entire clan who treats Mama as an outsider." Beitris shifted with a woeful sigh. "'Tis only the more vocal ones. Those able to stir the others and muddle their minds. Then the bad ones make the good ones wonder if they're wrong in trusting Mama." She pulled a sour face and lowered her voice. "Ye ken how it is. Always those ready to make trouble and bring out the worst in people. Especially after several lost their homes to the

English torches."

"We will protect yer mother," William said, rising to stand beside Valan. "Aye, Constable?"

Valan pointed at Beitris. "Guard this one with yer life," he ordered, then thumped William on the chest. "But dinna teach her any sword and spear tactics, ye ken?"

"Aye, m'lord." William appeared entirely too pleased with this latest assignment, but Valan would clarify his order at a later time.

"When is yer dung-heap of an uncle due to arrive?" he asked Beitris just as Dullis and a pair of maids entered with trays of food.

"Where be Lady Elspet?" Dullis sent a scowling glance around the room as she slid her tray onto the table.

"Gone to walk the battlements," Beitris said. She snatched up a double handful of bannocks and hurried to the door leading to the courtyard. "I shall take her these. Ye ken how she gets after every burning attempt on the village. Worries about letting down her guard."

"Why do ye no' take the tower stair?" Dullis jerked a stubby finger at the doorway at the back of the room.

"Looks to be a braw day," Beitris said. "I'll take the long way 'round and get a good stretch of my legs." She shot out the door, pausing only long enough to yank it shut behind her.

Valan gave William a subtle nod that sent him chasing after her.

"Ye're going to stand there and let him run after her like that?" Puffed with haughtiness, Dullis planted her knobby hands on her bony hips. "Do all yer warriors ignore yer commands?"

He would tolerate no more insolence from this woman. Especially since her loyalties reportedly lay with Euban. "Did yer mistress not command ye to be respectful?" He glowered at her, taking a step forward to add to the intended intimidation.

Dullis's eyes narrowed, and much to his surprise, she didn't appear fazed. "Aye, m'lord, but—"

He cut her off with an upward slice of his hand that nearly brushed her nose. "Silence!" The bellowed order echoed off the walls, adding to the effect he intended. "Lady Elspet ordered yer behavior changed. Either cede to yer mistress's wishes or another shall take yer place."

"She would never!"

Valan assumed a smug demeanor and allowed a moment of silence to strengthen his bluff. "Tell me, Dullis, did ye believe yer mistress would ever take a lover?"

The crone's mouth tightened. Her seething glower dropped as she shuffled back a step, displaying more humility and meekness than he had seen in her since his arrival. She nervously ran the tip of her tongue across her thin lips. "Forgive me, m'lord. The dangers to my mistress make me forget my place." After an awkward curtsy, she glanced back at the two maids standing behind her still holding their trays. "We have much food here, m'lord. Do ye wish to break yer fast here, or shall we take all of it back to the kitchens while ye join Lady Elspet on the battlements?"

The fact that the maid read his intentions so easily disturbed him. Made him decide not to underestimate her. The wily old woman might be more dangerous than she seemed. Perhaps a spy. Especially after what Beitris said about the woman's allegiance to Euban Maxwell. He selected a bannock, bit off a chunk, and stared at her as he chewed.

Dullis lifted her chin and waited. While somewhat meeker, her stubbornness and grit remained.

"Take the rest of the food to my knaves. They will see that it doesna go to waste." Although, knowing Marcas's contempt for anyone's cooking other than his own, the loyal servant would probably toss it to the chickens scratching around the courtyard.

"I shall see to it, m'lord." With a downward jerk of her chin, Dullis picked up her tray and glared at the other two maids to follow.

Valan waited until they left, then headed for the exit Elspet had used for her hasty departure. He pulled the door open and found himself in the northwest tower of the gatehouse, staring up at a spiral staircase of stone. With every step up the narrow, winding stairs, he became more determined to fend off Elspet's enemies.

When he emerged from the shadowy tower, he paused and allowed his eyes to adjust to the brightness of the rising sun. The view from the top of the imposing gatehouse was spectacular. All of Scotland seemed to spread out before him, or at least a good part of it. Verdant rolling hills. Clusters of trees here and there until they merged into a large wood surrounding what was left of the village. It was then he noticed the blackened remains of several buildings closest to the tree line. "Feckin' bastards."

"Over there is where we worked all our timber." Elspet appeared at his side, pointing at the charred remains farthest to the west. With a sweep of her hand, she pointed at the center of the ruins. "Then the dyeing and carding sheds were there. All filled with wool yet to be dyed and worked. Three dwellings farthest to the east and a small stable behind them." Seething rage flashed in her eyes and echoed in her voice. "They stole much, but at least they paid with a half dozen of their men." Jaw tensing, she shook her head. "It shouldha been much more." Her black hair whipped in the wind, streaming out like the wings of a dark angel.

Valan brushed it out of her eyes. "I will make the English pay for all they have cost ye...and more." Unable to resist, he moved behind her, combed her tresses back, and plaited them into a long, silky braid. With a hard yank, he broke free a leather tie from his chest plate and secured his handiwork.

Elspet examined the braid, then gifted him with a smile. "As good as any handmaid."

Her gaze rose to his long hair, most of it loose, other than the strands closest to his face. Those, he always pulled back and knotted at the back of his head to keep his view clear for battle.

"Yet, ye dinna plait yer own hair," she observed, then tossed the braid behind her shoulder. "Are all *Gallóglaigh* so talented?"

"I can only speak for myself, m'lady." He gave a modest bow, then tensed, remembering how he had learned the art of plaiting well enough to tend a lady's hair.

"Ahh...I see." Lady Elspet sauntered away from him. As she walked beside the wall, she allowed her fingers to graze across the tops of the merlons and down into the crenels. "Yer lady love taught ye how to braid her hair. Is that it?"

She had shared so much of her past with him. Perhaps it would be right to share his past with her. "Actually, it was my little sister," he said. "My mother had the household to care for along with a husband, three sons, and one wee daughter. Many were the time she wished aloud that God had given her more than two hands to accomplish all her tasks. It was a help to her when I plaited my sister's hair in the mornings."

Elspet turned and stared at him for a long while before responding, her expression unreadable. "Yer sister?" she repeated, almost as if she didn't believe him.

"Aye." He shook off the uncomfortable eeriness of speaking about it. Neither he nor his brothers ever spoke about their mother or sister. Their tragic deaths held too much pain.

"What happened to her?" Elspet stepped closer, a sympathetic knowing in her eyes. "I see suffering in yer eyes."

"An attack on our village while most of the men were on a hunt." He struggled to explain, immediately hating himself for raking open the old wound. Such a fool he was. What did he hope to gain by speaking of things better left unsaid?

"Who attacked?" she asked softly, resting her hand atop his.

"Mercenaries who claimed our chieftain had not paid them their due." The choking stench of burning flesh fouled his senses all over again. He snorted as he had done so many times before, but the nauseating smell always remained. "They raped every woman and child, impaled them, then set them on fire." He forced down the bile burning at the back of his throat. "They left one old woman alive enough to tell that it was them."

"God help ye." The horror in Elspet's face troubled him.

Sickening her had not been his intent.

"My brothers and I found every last one of them." He stared down at their hands resting together atop the stone wall. "We paid them their due." He took her hand and pressed a soft, lingering kiss to her knuckles. "Forgive me. I shouldha kept my past to myself. A lady such as yerself shouldna be burdened with such wickedness."

Her golden eyes shimmered with unshed tears, then she lunged and wrapped her arms around him, hugging him tight. "Dinna ask forgiveness. I am honored ye told me." She kissed his cheek, then leaned back, holding his face between her hands. "And it is my honor to help ye carry the burden of that terrible time." Her mouth trembled at the corners, her emotions fighting her effort to smile. "Ye listened to my memories. 'Tis only right I should listen to yers."

He wished they could stand like this forever, but that would not protect her. "Beitris told me about Euban."

She stiffened in his arms but didn't move away. "I see."

"And Granger," he added, determined to have no secrets between them.

This time, she stepped away. She turned to look out across her lands, squinting against the brilliance of the morning sun. "Apparently, my Beitris has outdone the maids when it comes to gossiping."

"It is nay gossip when it is true." Or at least, that was his opinion. "She worries for her mother and doesna wish to see her harmed."

"I dinna wish to see my daughter harmed either." Elspet scowled at the view, then motioned toward the horizon. With a long sweep of her hand, she encompassed all that lay before them. "This should belong to my Beitris. All of it. It is her right." Her hands closed into fists atop the chest-high opening in the stonework. "I dinna give a damn that she was born a lass, and neither did her father. Herbert often spoke of it when lamenting his inability to sire any more children." She turned and locked eyes with him. "Unfortunately, with Herbert dead, his brother is well within his rights to claim Caerlaverock and the lairdship." Bitterness crept into her tone. "I dinna care what Euban tries to do to me, but I will not allow him to harm my Beitris." With a hard glare, she proudly lifted her chin. "The last time he tried to touch her, I cut off his ear. If he tries again, I shall relieve him of his bollocks."

"A fair plan if ever I heard one." Valan moved to her side but refrained from touching her. "She said some in the clan are loyal to ye but most are not. Does she know of what she speaks?" Elspet did not deserve to be banished, or even worse—forced into a marriage with a bastard just to maintain her ties to the Maxwell clan and protect the people she cared about. As long as he drew breath, he would not allow such a terrible fate to befall her. When she failed to answer, he approached the dreaded issue another way. "How much sway do Euban and Granger truly hold?"

"More since Herbert's death." She gave a despondent thump of her fist atop the wall. "The clan gladly followed me in Herbert's stead whenever he was away. But now they tell me they wished Beitris had been born male to save them from Euban's cruel nature." She shook her head. "They know him to be a heartless cur, yet would follow him straight through the gates of Hell."

"None of the cowards will stand at yer side?"

"The women might. But verra few of the men. If any." She huffed out a disgusted laugh. "They have no issue with queens ruling in far-away lands but seem to believe a woman could never be a laird." A bitter smile curled her mouth. "Even though I have watched over them and helped them thrive for many a year now, they dinna feel I can manage the leadership of their clan."

Unfortunately, he knew she spoke the truth. While everyone easily accepted that the Lady Christiana had ruled the Lord of Argyll for years, should aught happen to their liege, the MacDougalls would replace him with the next male in line.

The same could be said about his own brother, Thorburn, former Constable over all the *Gallóglaigh*. Thorburn's wife, Adellis, not only ruled him but trained the *Gallóglaigh*'s finest archers. Yet if Thorburn should die before her, a new trainer would be found immediately.

"We men are fools," he admitted, scrubbing a hand along his jaw. "When is Euban due to arrive?"

"From what Beitris can find out, he will be here in three days' time."

"Then we shall be ready." He didn't know what or how, but he would see justice served.

The blaring blast of a horn from the northeastern tower took them both by surprise.

"God help us." Elspet pointed at the far side of the village. "They had no archers before today."

At the edge of the woods, the English dipped arrows into buckets of pitch, lit them, and released. The fiery missiles hit the thatched rooftops and quickly flared into an uncontrollable blaze.

Valan turned and ran to the side of the rooftop overlooking the inner courtyard. "To arms!" he bellowed. His order spread faster than the English's flames traveling through the thatch. His mighty warriors streamed out of both gates and headed for the foe. With a last glance at Elspet, he thumped his fist to his chest. "I will best these wrongs. I swear it."

And he would. No matter what it took.

CHAPTER FOUR

V ALAN'S HEART SANK when he found her kneeling in the smoldering ashes.

Face buried in her hands, her shoulders trembling, Elspet swayed from side to side, softly keening over all that had come to pass.

He flexed his burned, soot-covered hands, wishing for words to console her. None came. Castletoun was gone. Every dwelling, every workshop, either burned to the ground or transformed into a pitiful, blackened shell. He and his men had failed. Even though they had downed every archer before fighting to extinguish the fires, the enemy's pitch-coated arrows had accomplished their evil intent with deadly speed.

Still at a loss for what to say, he dropped down beside her and gathered her into his embrace.

Her quiet weeping became shuddering sobs. "All is gone," she cried. "All of it."

"I know, lass, I know." What else could he say? Aye, they could rebuild, but that would take time. More time than they had. Even though he didn't know the man, he felt sure Euban Maxwell would flaunt this as proof that the clan needed him as laird rather than Elspet or Beitris. "But yer people are safe. Every archer is dead, and my men are searching for the English's main camp to finish them off as well. They shall soon meet the justice of our blades."

After a while, she grew still, only shifting with an occasional hiccupping sniff. Her heartbreaking sobs ceased, but her quiet weeping continued. Silent tears, now. Tears that tore at his heart and soul.

"It is too late," she whispered. "I have lost it all. The people will never follow Beitris now."

"Nay, ye have protected Caerlaverock. All the Maxwell lands. All is not lost." He pressed his cheek to the top of her head, ignoring the men, women, and children sifting through the smoking rubble around them. "Dinna give up, Elspet. It isna in ye to do so."

"It is now." She pushed away from him and stood. With a swipe of her hand, she smeared the sooty blackness across her cheeks. After a despondent look all around, she slowly shook her head. A weariness, an expression of disbelief puckered her grimy brow. "I never thought Herbert's many campaigns would ever provoke such a heartless attack against us. Not here." She sniffed again. "Apparently, I underestimated the power of hatred and greed."

Valan stood. He had to think of a way to help her. It pained him to see her this way.

"M'lady, we have lost everything." A barefoot man covered in the filth of the charred remains stumbled toward them. He hugged an arm around his pregnant wife, helpless to console her.

"Even the bairn's cradle is gone." The distraught young mother's voice broke, tears streaming from her red-rimmed eyes. "Angus's Da made it afore he died. Now we've nothing to remember him by."

"I know some things canna be replaced," Elspet said. "Please, I beg yer forgiveness." She reached for them, but they shied away, shunning her. Condemnation filled their eyes. Elspet wept harder.

Valan steadied her, wrapping an arm around her waist, should she go limp and start to fall. He held her close and called out what little solace he could give to the desperate couple. "Ye willna be without a roof or food while yer home is rebuilt.

Caerlaverock will house everyone as long as need be, ye ken? Lady Elspet will see to it that all are provided for. As she always has. Ye know that, aye?"

They didn't speak. Instead, just managed a vague nod and wandered away, staring at the ground as they weaved their way through the destruction.

"God forgive me for failing them." Elspet watched them leave, her fists clutched to her chest.

"Ye havena failed anyone." Valan stepped in front of her and took her by the shoulders. He refused to allow her hopelessness to pull her any lower. She had to fight. There was no other choice. "The only way ye might fail them is to give up now." He jutted his chin at the collapsed dwelling beside them. "Mourn the losses, aye, do that. Ye should. But yer people need yer courage now more than ever. *Things* were lost. But all yer people still live. In that, ye should be proud." He leaned closer, bending to level his gaze with hers. "And ye are not alone in this. I am at yer side and there, I shall say. Understand?"

She stared at him as though trapped in a trance. A hint of a smile curved her mouth. "I am glad for yer presence, but I dinna ken how ye can help us further." A woefulness filled her voice, making it tremble. "Ousting the English is only part of the battle." After a weary shake of her head, she added, "I fear ye canna help with Euban claiming his place as laird and tormenting us even more."

"We have three days to prepare for the bastard's arrival." He rubbed his burning eyes, gritty and dry from the smoky air. With a snort to clear his nostrils of the stench, he curled an arm around her and steered her toward the gatehouse. "Come. We can do no more here."

She stood fast. "I must stay and help them sort through and clear away that which canna be saved."

"Nay, m'lady." With a gentle but firm pull, he moved her along beside him. "Ye havena eaten or rested in too long. How can ye plan a successful campaign when ye are exhausted and

48

weak from hunger?"

Her befuddled expression confirmed his suspicions. She needed to eat and rest. "See? Ye canna even come up with an argument." He nudged her along like a mother hen herding chicks.

Her confused look became a scowl, and she pushed away, coming to a hard stop. "I must help my people."

"Ye can help yer people by bathing away the darkness of this day, having a meal, then going to bed. After ye've rested, we shall plan Euban Maxwell's permanent departure from Caerlaverock." He kept her walking, holding her tightly to keep her from falling. She stumbled along like one who couldn't see past their own inner turmoil. But he would get her through this. Her will to fight would return with food and rest.

When they reached the gatehouse, the two elderly guards clamped their mouths shut and turned aside as if Lady Elspet no longer deserved their respect. Valan resolved to speak with them later. Their loyalties needed guidance. They would support their courageous Lady of Caerlaverock if he had to beat respect into them.

William and Beitris waited just inside the entrance to the courtyard. Their faces reflected the grimness of the situation.

Beitris rushed to her mother's side and slid beneath her arm to support her. "Come, Mama. I'm sure Dullis already has the laundress boiling the water for yer bath. We'll get ye cleaned, fed, filled with whisky broth, and off to yer dreams, aye?" She shot a determined glare back at Valan as she led Elspet away.

"We must talk," Valan said to William as he watched Elspet climb the forestair and enter her private hall. "We have but three days to come up with a plan that doesna include killing Euban and Granger."

"Even an accident wouldna be acceptable?" William's eyes narrowed to plotting slits. He stared off into the distance and scratched the reddish-blond stubble shadowing his jaw.

Valan debated the possibility, warming to William's suggestion. "Another course of action would be better, I think. With but three days to prepare, it would be a challenge to arrange two believable accidents—one for Euban and one for Granger." He scanned the courtyard, idly noting any possibilities that might help rid them of one or both men. A fall from the battlements might be difficult to manage without witnesses. "Lady Elspet must be above reproach. Therefore, we must strive to be the same, since I am sure her enemies have noted our loyalty to her."

"She and her husband were always loyal to the king, aye?" William's blue eyes flashed, a sure sign the young warrior had come up with a different tactic.

"Aye. Loyal to Alexander and Scotland both." A subtle survey of the courtyard revealed entirely too many folk who might overhear. "Come." Valan moved them to the forestair, pausing on the landing in the first turn. There, they would be too high to be heard from below, and safe from anyone approaching without their knowledge. "What is yer plan?"

"Did the MacDougall happen to share the name of my cousin with ye?" William shifted in place as though embarrassed to ask the question.

Valan didn't care about the man's lineage, but William behaved as though it was important. "Not a word of it. He told us of yer warring skills when ye showed up five years ago determined to join the *Gallóglaigh*. Yer ancestry was of no concern to us."

William's grip on the wooden railing tightened, turning his knuckles white. "I gave my name as MacAlpine." He paused, tilting his head as if that should mean something.

"Aye, what of it? Out with it, man. This is no time for guessing games." Valan glanced up at the door to Elspet's private hall. Not a single servant had entered or exited. Beitris should have sent for food and wine for her mother by now.

"MacAlpine is actually one of my middle names. De Coucy is my surname."

"William MacAlpine de Coucy?" The hairs rose on the back of Valan's neck. He studied the lad closer. "Are ye saying ye are a relation of our king?" With William's reddish-blond hair and massive build, Valan found that hard to believe.

His second in command twitched a nervous shrug. "A cousin, actually. A distant one. But Alexander and I have always maintained a verra close accord. He granted me permission to join the Lord of Argyll's *Gallóglaigh* out of deference to my mother. She and his mother, Marie de Coucy, have always been close as well." He squared his broad shoulders. "No one but yerself and the Lord of Argyll knows of this, though. Thankfully, both Alexander and the MacDougall agreed to set aside the old grievances regarding the previous Lord of Argyll's allegiance to Norway and Alexander's father's death at Kerrera whilst attempting to bring them back to Scotland."

Valan leaned back against the sturdy wood railing and scrubbed his face with both hands. "God's teeth, man, ye didna think to share this with me 'til now?"

"I wished no special treatment."

"The only special treatment ye wouldha received was yer arse sent back to yer mother and yer cousin." He glared at the young warrior who was about ten years his junior. A brother in arms who had battled harder than all the rest to achieve the coveted position of second in command of the mighty *Gallóglaigh*.

"A man has no control over his ancestry, Constable. Only his future."

True. Valan held his tongue and stepped aside as a pair of maids scurried up the steps, squeezed past them, then entered Elspet's hall. One carried a tray of food. The other clutched a bucket in one hand and a pitcher in the other. 'Twas about time they tended their mistress. His gaze slid back to William. Now. What to do about this one? Such connections could easily become a royal pain in the arse.

"I have an idea that might help," William offered.

"What?"

"Alexander should be in Fife this time of year. At Kinghorn Castle, ye ken?" William paused as if that information would somehow deliver Caerlaverock from Euban's clutches.

Valan failed to see how. Fife was north of the Firth of Forth, well across it in fact, beyond Edinburgh. "And?" Damn, the boy had a way of dragging out what was on his mind. "Out with it!"

"We could send word. Request he name Lady Elspet the laird and place the Maxwell lands safely under her protection." He almost bounced in place, unable to contain his excitement.

Valan held up three fingers. "We have only three short days 'til Euban arrives. There is not a horse alive that can get all the way to Kinghorn and back here in three days." He let his hand drop and shook his head. "And I verra much doubt our king would take such a political risk as issuing a command that Lady Elspet be made Clan Maxwell's next laird. Gifts of manors, holdings, and lands to a woman is one thing. Giving her control of a clan, especially one so close to the border, is another thing entirely. He willna risk that. There is enough turmoil already between the families of Scotland."

William scowled up at the hall's door as if it was the source of the problem. "Then I dinna have a feckin' clue about what might be done."

"Come. We will join the women and speak with them." Valan climbed the stairs, then turned back and studied William. Another plan came to him, falling in place like well-woven chainmail. The young warrior liked Beitris well enough. Seemed besotted with her, even. Surely, the men of Clan Maxwell would covet a connection to the king of Scotland. Respect it, even. What clan wouldn't desire such a powerful laird?

"Why do ye stare at me?" William squinted and braced himself, as though expecting a blow to the jaw.

"Ye find yerself drawn to Lady Beitris, aye?"

One of William's brows inched higher than the other. "Perhaps—why?"

Valan almost laughed out loud at the man's leeriness. "A marriage to the king's cousin with the condition that Caerlaverock and all the Maxwell lands be the lady's dowry would be difficult for Euban and Granger to challenge."

"M-marriage?"

"Since when do ye stutter?"

"I started stuttering when ye decided I should marry." William shook his head. "I canna marry. I am a…a warrior."

"Have ye forgotten my brothers? Thorburn and Ross?" Valan leaned against the railing and waited. "Both are still respected *Gallóglaigh* constables even though Thorburn concentrates on training new men, while Ross recruits and negotiates the most profitable campaigns. Both are married with children." He climbed the last few steps and stopped again just outside the door. "Consider it, aye? 'Twould be a reasonable enough solution, and one that would be difficult for Euban to fight without looking like a traitor to his king."

"I-I will consider it."

Valan doubted it. The man had gone pale. Perhaps he had nay been as besotted with the Lady Beitris as Valan believed. He shouldered open the heavy door to the hall, then came to an abrupt stop just across the threshold. Elspet and Beitris sat at one end of the long oak table eating in silence. They had washed the battle's grime from their hands, but their faces and everything else were still coated in soot.

Elspet eyed him over the rim of her goblet, then slowly lowered it to the table. "What has come to pass now?"

With a wave for William to keep up, Valan strode across the room and joined them at the table. He seated himself on the end of the bench closest to Elspet. "Nothing, m'lady. Dinna fash yerself." He looked to William and then directed his attention to the long cabinet opposite the wide hearth on the other side of the room. It was filled with pitchers, decanters, goblets, and tankards. "Pour us a drink, aye?" He hoped that assigning the man a task would enable the young warrior to rid himself of that hunted look.

"Aye, Constable." William hurried across the room, his hands tensing into fists, then relaxing as if he battled with himself.

Beitris watched him, frowning. She leaned forward and whispered, "What is wrong with him? He looks like a deer that just spotted the hounds."

Valan waved her words aside. "Nothing is amiss, Lady Beitris. I assure ye." He returned his attention to Elspet and tapped a finger on the grubby forearm of her armor. "I thought bathing and fresh clothes wouldha come first."

"With all the ash and soot in my hair, Dullis decided a full bath was in order." She pushed the platter of cheeses and apples closer to him along with the plate of bread. A sigh escaped her as she rubbed her eyes. "It takes a while to heat enough water to fill the tub in the corner of my chambers."

"Da brought it to her all the way from the Holy Land." Beitris poured more wine into her mother's goblet and then refilled her own. "'Tis a fine thing of copper with a fancy rolled rim. And special soaps with a recipe for how to make more, too. Caitra's mother is the washerwoman, and ye canna tell the difference between the soaps she makes and the ones Da brought back from his travels."

"Aye, but it takes so much work to fill the monstrous thing, I usually settle for a simple washing in the basin each day." Elspet pushed her plate aside and sagged back in her chair. "But it was a thoughtful gift." Resting her head in her hand, her weary look turned thoughtful and sad. "Herbert was a kind man. Sure to be missed."

"He would nay have to be missed if he had stayed here where he was needed." Beitris banged her metal goblet on the table.

"Dinna speak ill of the dead." Elspet forced herself to sit straighter, but worry still slumped her shoulders.

Valan downed the whisky William set in front of him, then helped himself to the cheese and bread. After a side-eyed glance at William, he decided to help the marriageable warrior come to the appropriate conclusion. "William and I have come up with a way to foil Euban and Granger."

"Without killing them?" Elspet might be tired, but the firm

insistence in her voice remained strong. She locked her pointed glare on him.

"Without killing them," he repeated.

Beitris stabbed a slice of apple as if it was one of the men in question. "Would the clan not be better off without both of them?"

"Aye," Elspet said. "But I fear many in our clan dinna realize that. We can ill afford any accusations of murder. Especially with the village gone. We are mere women, remember?"

"There is nothing *mere* about either of ye." Valan reached for the decanter of whisky, then gave his second in command a meaningful nudge. "Tell them our idea, William. See what they think." 'Twas time the warrior realized the needs of an entire clan far outweighed the needs of one *Gallóglaigh*.

"I am...uhm...King Alexander's cousin." William stared down at the table, his body tensed tighter than a newly strung bow. He slid his glass back and forth between his hands, nervously tapping it with his fingers. "If the Lady Beitris weds me, with the condition that Caerlaverock and all Maxwell lands are her dowry, not only would the men of the clan most likely accept us as the new laird and lady, but Euban couldna fight it out of fear of looking a traitor."

"Yer enthusiasm for this plan makes my heart pound, William." Beitris's words dripped with sarcasm. She gave a disgusted shake of her head and stabbed another slice of apple.

Elspet's sleek, dark brows rose to her hairline. "And I assume Euban would be told that the king himself demanded such a dowry for consent to marry his cousin?"

"Absolutely." Valan lifted his glass for a toast. "Do ye not think it a solid plan?"

"Would proof not be required?" Elspet leaned forward, her interest piqued. "An order bearing King Alexander's seal?"

"Aye." William perked up as if sensing salvation at hand.

"Ye dinna have to be such an arse about it," Beitris snapped. "Ye liked me well enough earlier today. Enough to steal a kiss."

Valan slowly shifted on the bench and faced William. "Steal a kiss, she says? Even after my order that the women of Clan Maxwell were to remain untouched?"

"I nay succeeded."

"That is not the point."

Elspet smacked the table. "I am too tired to listen to the two of ye bicker like a pair of spoiled bairns. If William doesna wish to marry, then another plan must be found." She blew out a disgusted huff, pushed back her chair, and stood. "I am going to see how much water is ready. Settle this amongst yerselves and let me know whether Beitris and I should start packing our things." She paused at the doorway to her chambers and bowed her head. "And while ye're at it, any suggestions on where we might go would be much appreciated. Since I know of no one who will take us in." Without another word, she left and closed the door softly behind her.

"There has to be someone who would take ye in." William cast a worried look at Beitris.

"Who?" She poured herself more wine and scowled at him over the rim. "My father's only kin is Euban. All my mother's kin banished us. They've never even met me." She took a long slow sip, then shrugged. "Except for the Lady Christiana. She is the only ally my mother has. Why do ye think the Lord of Argyll bade ye come to us so quickly?"

"And how do ye think the Lady of Argyll will react when word reaches her that ye refused to help her kin?" Valan turned to William. Victory was near. The snare had been set and nearly sprung. All they need do now was collect their trophy.

"I did not refuse," William said. "Exactly."

"Neither did ye volunteer willingly," Beitris shot back at him with a hard narrowing of her eyes. "I ken well enough I am nay exactly the wifely type, but I promise ye would never suffer any boredom." She rose, dismissing both the subject and William with a careless flip of her hand. "I am off to the battlements for air." She paused and glared back at them, flaring her delicate nostrils. "The stench of cowardice is strong in this room. 'Tis about to choke me." She slammed the door to the tower stair so hard, the flames danced across the five-armed candelabra.

"Well done, William." Valan poured another whisky, waiting for his second in command to say the words he wanted to hear.

"They truly have nowhere to go?" William asked quietly. "Truly?"

Valan shook his head. "The MacDougall would probably allow us to bring them back to Argyll, but I doubt verra much that Lady Christiana would be pleased with that solution. After all, if Lady Beitris had been born a man, the lairdship of the clan would be hers without question, creating another powerful ally in the borderlands for Clan MacDougall. But as it is, if Clan Maxwell is lost to Euban, rumor has it his loyalties lie with whoever benefits him most. I wouldna be surprised if he is not the one responsible for the English attacks on Caerlaverock."

"What a bastard." William stared down into his empty glass.

Valan refilled their glasses and lifted his for a toast. "The decision is ultimately yers, William. But I advise ye to think long and hard and let yer conscience be yer guide. Ye can claim a lairdship, a wife, and be the savior of a clan or doom these innocent folk to the cruel leadership of Euban Maxwell and turn Lady Elspet and Lady Beitris into a pair of homeless women forced to do whatever necessary to survive."

"That is not fair."

"Life rarely is." Valan downed the whisky and set his glass on the table. He pushed himself to his feet, strolled to the door leading to Elspet's private chambers, then paused and turned a steely glare on William. "I want an answer from ye by daybreak. That is an order. Not a request. And if ye fail to keep *that* order, I shall leave it to my blade to handle any further discussion. Understood?"

"Aye, Constable."

The door flew open just as he reached for the latch.

"Saint's bones!" Startled, Dullis dropped Elspet's soiled armor and clutched her chest. She bobbed up and down, scooping up the articles one by one. With an insolent sneer, she blocked his way. "Her ladyship is bathing and wants solitude."

"I shall wash her back. On wi' ye now." He had no time for the surly maid and trusted her even less. When William came to his senses and agreed to marry Beitris, the details of the union, including the procurement of a proper forgery of the king's order, would have to be launched with the stealth and precision of a battle ambush to keep the maid from betraying them.

When the crone refused to move, he set her aside and pointed toward the dining hall's outer exit. "I said *on wi' ye*, Dullis. Challenging me is ill-advised, and if ye persist in doing so, I shall order my men to pack ye up and deliver ye to Euban Maxwell afore the sun sets."

The older woman's eyes flared wide. She backed away, then scurried off, her lopsided veil flopping like the wings of a great white bird.

Good. 'Twas high time the crone realized her loyalties were known. He closed the outer door, headed down the hallway, and entered the small sitting room next to Elspet's bedchamber. His intentions were two-fold: discover if the lady found Beitris's marriage to William acceptable, and, as he had told Dullis, help the lovely lass with her bathing.

He eased open the bedchamber door, noting the dimness of the room. The maid must have drawn the tapestries across the windows to grant the lady a wee bit of peace and privacy. The hinges creaked, revealing his progress as he entered.

"Dullis, please. I said I wished to be alone."

"It is not Dullis." He closed the door behind him and settled the bar across it.

"Valan." She sounded neither surprised nor irritated. A very encouraging sign, indeed.

"Aye, m'lady." He stepped around the wooden screen and came to halt, helpless to avert his hungry stare.

Candles cast a golden glow throughout the bathing alcove,

the reflections of the flames dancing across the burnished edges of the hammered copper tub. Submerged in rose-scented milkiness, the waterline rippling just above her breasts, Elspet reclined in one end of the large tub with her arms resting atop its flared sides. Apparently, she had already washed her hair. Sleek and shining, it flowed down into the water, a river of purest ebony.

"Ye are a goddess," he whispered, frozen in place.

She smiled and closed her eyes, pillowing her head on a folded linen propped behind her. "Nay, my fine accomplice. I am merely a woman trying to survive my time allotted on this earth."

"Accomplice?" He yanked at the endless straps securing his armor in place. "Accomplice in what, dear Elspet?"

She didn't bother opening her eyes, just softly laughed and rolled her head back and forth on the pillow of linen. "Dinna go coy on me now, Valan." Her long dark lashes fluttered as she opened her eyes the barest slit. "Let there only be truth between us, aye? Always."

"Always, my own." He shed his armor, chainmail, and hauberk, dropping them to the floor as he peeled them off. For good measure, especially since she didn't seem averse to his presence, he kicked off his boots but decided to wait on removing his trews. Details needed to be addressed before pleasure. "It is my hope the plan of William marrying Beitris nay offended ye."

"It did not." She submerged her hands and recovered a small cloth from the depths of the steaming water.

As she dribbled a trail of water up her arms and across her front, Valan recanted his previous decision and stripped off his trews to keep his hardness from overstraining the seams.

"And I dinna believe it offended my Beitris either." Her mouth curled into a suggestive grin. "I am certain Beitris finds William much more suitable than the older men who have expressed interest in her." Her sultry gaze shifted from her bathing to him. "There is room in here for both of us, fine sir." Then she feigned a sad shake of her head. "Alas, though. If ye remember, our boons are paid in full."

"Our boons will never be paid in full, m'lady." And he meant every word. But as he went to step into the tub, she held up a hand and stopped him.

"The matter of marriage must be settled first." She scooted higher, allowing her dark nipples to peek above the water.

"Our marriage?" God's beard, had he actually said, *Our marriage*? The dangerous words had sprung from him without his permission.

Her head shifted to a curious tip, and both her brows rose as high as they could go. She stared at him for a long moment. "Our marriage?" she repeated.

He resettled his footing. Suddenly unsure what to do with his hands, he folded his arms across his bare chest. What the hell was wrong with him? He was nay such a coward. It was then he realized why the words had slipped from his tongue. Because he had meant them. Aye, she was his. For now and always. He lifted his chin, assuming a self-assured attitude he didn't quite feel—yet. But it would come.

"Aye. Our marriage," he confirmed, bracing himself for her reaction.

"I was speaking of William and Beitris. The lad did not seem inclined to agree with the plan. I will not allow my Beitris united with a man who will resent her and possibly treat her ill."

The infernal woman acted as if he had not just offered for her. A frustrated snort huffed free of him. "One union at a time, woman. What about ours?"

CHAPTER FIVE

O F ALL THE things Elspet expected from Valan, an offer of marriage was not one of them. And he had done it by accident. Perhaps too much whisky and too little food were responsible. She assumed a firm yet kind tone. "I spent a lifetime married to a warrior who was never with me. A *lonely* lifetime. Why would I wish for another such union?"

The intensity of his gaze made her heart pound. With some difficulty, she reminded herself he had misspoken. The proof of it had shone in his face as soon as the words left his lips. Pure shock had flashed in his eyes, bright as lightning. It was the whisky. Or the candlelight. Maybe even the rose petals scenting the steam. Or most likely the weariness and frustration about the day's losses twisting his words in a way he hadn't intended. Aye, he had not meant to propose marriage, but now the poor man didn't know how to remain chivalrous *and* retract the offer.

She forced a light-heartedness, even though a heavy sense of disappointment filled her, a sinking feeling that refused to be ignored. "Admit it, fine sir. Ye nay meant to say *our marriage*. Ye surprised yerself when ye said it. I saw it plain as day. Only truth between us—remember? Besides, what does a mighty *Gallóglaigh* need with a wife?"

After another disgruntled snort, he climbed into the tub and eased down into the water. "God's beard, this is hot."

"Of course, it's hot. They boil the water down below and

hoist it up in the buckets attached to that chain. Herbert saw something like it during his travels and ordered it built when he brought the tub home." The sturdy chain was suspended from an iron hook embedded in one of the great beams supporting the ceiling. It disappeared down into a hole in the floor behind the tub and ended in the bathing room below. There, water was boiled not only for the washing of bodies but also for washing clothes.

"By the time the servants hauled the water up using the outer stair, it grew tepid far too soon. Herbert's discovery not only made it easier for them but provided the hottest water for the bath." Saints help her, she had succumbed to nervous blethering. If that didn't distract him from the course he had accidentally taken, she would drive it from his mind with seduction. The wickedness of enjoying him in the water made her ache with anticipation.

Gradually, he relaxed, stretching out his long, muscular legs on either side of hers and resting back against his end of the tub. "I meant every word I said. I wish ye to be my wife, Elspet."

"Why?"

He reached under the water, took hold of her ankles, and propped her legs on top of his. With a masterful touch, he stroked her calves, inching higher with every caress. "What do ye mean *why?*"

"'Tis a simple enough word, Valan." Arguing with the man was almost impossible with him touching her that way. "Why do ye wish me to be yer wife?"

He stared at her. Even by the softness of the candlelight, she recognized the worry and uncertainty puckering his brow.

She scooted closer, shifted to her knees, and rested her hands on his shoulders. "I know ye didna mean to say it," she breathed into his ear, teasing with her closeness. "And it is all right. I dinna hold ye to it." After a tender kiss to assure him no ill feelings stood between them, she reached down, filled her cupped hand with water, then let it trickle down his chest. "Let me bathe ye, my fine one. Wash away our worries and enjoy this time together."

He caught hold of both her wrists and held her captive. Jaw flexing, he slowly shook his head. "Nay, my own. Not until we settle this matter between us." The deep richness of his voice held no regret or uncertainty now, only determination. "I willna lie. I did surprise myself." Bringing her right hand forward, he pressed a kiss into her palm. It sent such a surge of heat through her, 'twas a wonder she didn't burst into flames. "But as soon as I heard the words aloud, I knew them for the truth of my heart." He treated her left palm to a kiss just as heated, tickling the tip of his tongue to the ends of her fingers. "I want ye as my wife, Elspet, and I swear, I shall never leave ye wondering if I will ever return."

While she wanted to believe him, how could his oath be true? "Ye are a mercenary by trade. Yer life is travel and living by the sword." Even though his hold was still snug on her wrists, she framed his face between her hands. "Only truth between us, Valan. Only truth. Warring is in yer blood. And do ye truly think the Lord of Argyll will allow the commander of his men to settle down and take up sheep herding? Or farming?" She didn't wish to be cruel, but he needed to see sense to escape any false hopes for a life together. "And I wager ye dinna even have a home. Or land. Why would ye? Would it truly satisfy ye to spend our future here with Laird William and Lady Beitris? I think not."

He released her wrists and pulled her across him as he leaned back against the end of the tub. The hard length of him pressed against her belly as he slicked his hands from her shoulders down to her buttocks. "I have land," he whispered into her hair, filling his hands with her rear and squeezing. "I even have a title although it escapes me at the moment." He pulled her higher, kissed a trail between her breasts, then moved to her nipples. "But none of that matters," he said, sliding into her with a slow, smooth shove. "All that matters is I want ye for my wife. The mother of my children. The one I wake to each day, and I fall asleep beside each night. It can be done, my own, even with me being a commander of such a great and mighty army. My brothers have done it. I will do it, too." He slid his hands up her back and filled them with her hair. With a gentle pull, he tilted her face up to his and locked his gaze with hers. "Say yes, Elspet. I beg ye—and I am nay a man who begs for anything." The water sloshed as he increased the rhythm of his steady in and out thrusting. "Elspet," he rasped. "What say ye?"

The warm, scented waves rolled back and forth against her sides and splashed across her back with every wondrous thrust. Even with him deep inside her, teetering on the pinnacle of ecstasy, she had to know before shuddering bliss took her to the point of telling him anything he wanted to hear. "Why, Valan?"

"Because ye are mine," he growled, spinning with her in the oversized tub and settling her back against the reclining end. "Mine," he repeated, driving into her. Water splashed and slopped over the sides. "Mine to have. To protect. To love." He shoved in deep and held fast, bringing his mouth close to hers. "Say yes, damn ye. Yes, to all that a future together could hold for us."

"Yes," she gasped. This was madness for certain, but how could she refuse him? The decision made, she gave over to the delicious sensations refusing to remain second to conversation any longer. "Yes, Valan!" she said much louder, but for a very different reason.

Her answer appeared to feed his already raging drive to possess her. He surged like a great sea god determined to show her the wonders of pleasuring in the water. She arched upward, shattering into shards of pure rapture.

Valan's unearthly roar quickly followed, echoing off the sides of the copper tub. He collapsed into her arms and pressed his forehead against hers. "I fear I have greatly decreased our water level, m'lady," he gasped, still struggling to catch his breath.

"A good thing," she murmured, then pressed a kiss to his temple. "If not, I wouldha surely drowned."

His deep laugh rumbled between them. He lifted his head and stared into her eyes. "Ye meant it, aye?"

"Aye," she said, still fighting her fears and worries. She touched his cheek. Gently. Fearfully.

Even in the candlelight, the man missed nothing. Brow furrowing, he drew so close, she thought she would surely drown in the blue of his eyes. "What is it, my own?"

She didn't answer. Couldn't.

"Elspet. Tell me." He turned them in the tub again, sloshing out even more water. Gathering her atop him, he settled her so her head rested in the dip of his shoulder. "I see it in yer eyes, dear one. What troubles ye?"

"We have known each other but a little while." That wasn't what truly worried her, but perhaps it would be a good enough reason so he wouldn't keep after her. She wished more water remained. Even though it was summer, the air against her damp skin felt too cool. "We should move closer to the fire." She pushed up to climb out of the tub.

He caught hold of her arm and held her fast. "Truth, Elspet. Always truth between us, remember?"

With a smile, she bowed her head and released a heavy sigh. "We have already spoken of it, my fine sir. I fear only time will bring me the reassurance I need. Ye have reassured me as much as ye can. Now, I must live it to believe it, ye ken?"

His hand slipped away from her. "Ye fear being abandoned. Left alone again."

She climbed out of the tub, hurried around the screen, and over to the hearth to wrap herself in the linen cloth Dullis had hung there to warm. "There is another drying cloth hanging beside the chain. Do ye see it?" After wrapping the soft weave around her body, she secured it with a firm tuck under her arm. Coming back around the screen, she held up the cloth as she padded through the puddles. "The maids willna be pleased. We have covered the floor with water."

"I have noticed something about ye." He rose from the tub

and distracted her with a magnificent view of his fine taut buttocks as he reached for the cloth on the peg.

"What is that?"

"Ye try to distract me when ye dinna wish to discuss what ye truly feel." He wrapped the linen around his trim waist and knotted it at the side. He came to a standstill in one of the larger puddles spreading across the bedchamber floor. "I willna hurt ye, Elspet. Not ever. Do ye think ye will ever come to trust what I tell ye?"

She went to him, took hold of his little finger, and led him to stand with her by the fire. How could she make him understand? "Harping on and on about my fears and what caused them does little to make them go away." She leaned close and kissed his wet shoulder. "Time and experience are what I need to wipe away my doubts, ye ken?"

He gathered her into his arms and kissed her with such fierce protectiveness, she had to clutch him to keep from falling. "We will make our happiness," he promised when he lifted his mouth from hers. "Ye will see."

It was then she noticed some of the day's grubbiness still clinging to his face. It brought her a smile. She ran a fingertip through one of the sootier spots and showed it to him. "Ye distracted me, so I failed to notice ye needed a wash as badly as I did."

With a devilish look, he dropped the cloth to the floor, proudly baring himself and revealing his renewed hardness. "Perhaps I should return to the water, m'lady. Care to join me?"

"Ye may join me in the bed, my fine lover. *After* ye have washed." To provide incentive, she let her wrap fall away, sauntered across the room, and seductively situated herself among the pillows.

When he took a step in her direction, she held up a finger and shook it. "Nay, m'love. Wash first."

His victorious smile made her realize what she had just called him. Apparently, Valan wasn't the only one in this room who had little control over his tongue. With a failed attempt at looking stern, she pointed at the bathing area.

After a self-satisfied tip of his head, he disappeared back behind the screen. A great deal of splashing told her an ample amount of water remained for his needs.

"Ye dinna have to worry about William," he called out from behind the screen. "The lad has a good conscience and during our five years of fighting together, I have never seen a hint of cruelty in him."

"Fighting together is not the same as marriage." Although, she supposed it could be, knowing Beitris's temper. "I want my daughter happy in this union as well as in overseeing these lands that are rightfully hers." She sat up and leaned over, combing her fingers through her wet hair. 'Twould be a wavy mess without combing it dry in front of the fire. The thought made her smile. Wavy hair was a small price to pay for an afternoon in Valan's arms. "Do ye think the things I said before leaving the room filled him with enough guilt to do as we wish?"

Valan laughed. "Sly minx. I wondered about that desperate speech ye gave." More splashing followed by a loud snorting. Poor man must have gotten water, soap, or both up his nose.

"So, it moved him?" She cocked an ear, hoping for the right answer. She had never attempted to portray herself as pitiful or victimized.

"I feel sure he will come 'round." Valan emerged from behind the screen, the hard planes of his muscular body taking on a golden sheen in the candlelight. With the linen cloth, he squeezed water from his hair, then scrubbed the wetness from his body. "I ordered him to give us an answer by dawn. That gives his conscience ample time to push him in the right direction."

He tossed the linen aside and joined her in the bed. "All will be well," he promised, nuzzling the tender flesh behind her ear and smoothing his warm, large hand down her side and up between her thighs.

"All will be well, indeed." She arched into his touch and concentrated on the moment's pleasures, refusing to allow her worries to spoil it. Whatever was meant to happen would happen—whether her worries led the way or not.

VALAN PEERED CLOSER at the forged stamp. His weaponry knave had carved an amazing amount of detail into the end of an appropriately sized oak stick. An image of the king, holding his sword and scepter while seated on the throne. The intricate scene was surrounded by decorative beading and several words Valan couldn't make out since he always struggled with Latin. It was an exact replica of King Alexander's privy seal. Used to authenticate official documents of a more personal nature to His Majesty. "How did Niall come to know so much about the king's privy seal?"

"I did not ask, m'lord." Marcas gave a meaningful nod toward the creation. "As the provisions knave, I never question the weaponry knave's work just as he never questions my healing or cooking." He offered a folded parchment with a proud smile. "I handled the writing of the order. Make quite the scribe if I say so m'self." He tapped a finger on the wooden stamp. "I have the sealing wax ready to light if everything meets yer approval."

Valan carefully opened the order, noting the folded edges of the parchment had been rubbed until worn. The lightly frayed edges added authenticity. As though the thing had passed through several hands and traveled a long distance in the messenger's pouch. As he moved closer to the candle and read the forgery, the skills of his two knaves not only made him smile but also appreciate that they served him and not someone else. He handed it back to Marcas. "Well done. Impressive work from the both of ye. Even better than I hoped."

"Roland waits to pose as the messenger." Marcas refolded the parchment, dripped a glob of honey-colored wax on the flap, and embossed it with the seal. "Since he and Master Artan were among those who left to level the English's camp, verra few have seen his face—especially no one who might reveal that he's nay a true messenger for the king."

"Niall and yerself have served me well indeed." Valan clapped a hand on the man's shoulder. "As ye always do." He cracked open the door of the small storage room and peeked out. No one must see either him or Marcas. He tossed a glance back over his shoulder. "'Tis safe to go. Stealth now, Marcas. No one must find any evidence, ye ken?"

Marcas smiled, tucked the order inside his tunic, and picked up the small iron chamberstick with its sputtering candle. "Dinna fash yerself, m'lord. I shall toss the stamp into the first roaring hearth I pass. Roland waits for me at the edge of the woods outside the postern gate. He knows to bide his time for a bit then deliver the message to Lady Elspet in front of witnesses."

"Good. On wi' ye then." He stepped back, allowing Marcas to leave first. While giving the knave enough time to put some distance between himself and the storage room, he ran through the details of their plan yet again. They could leave nothing to chance. He stood in the darkness, studying it from every angle. As of yet, he found no glaring issues they might have missed. After ample time passed, he placed his ear to the door and listened. Nothing but silence came from the passage running between the southeastern tower and the great banquet hall attached to the back skirting wall. With stealth perfected from endless battles, he slipped out, hurried down the hall, and entered the courtyard with no one's notice.

He needed to find William and update him on how the message would be delivered. With any hope, his second in command had settled his uneasiness after his nervous announcement that he would, in fact, take the Lady Beitris for his wife. Beitris had rolled her eyes but agreed. God help William MacAlpine de Courcy. Valan smiled at a sudden realization. If the daughter was anything like the mother, the young warrior would soon discover himself a very lucky man indeed.

Movement at the top of the forestair across the courtyard caught his eye. Elspet emerged, pausing on the landing to make a slow perusal of the area. Rather than armor, she wore a deep blue gown that somehow made her even lovelier. The close-fitting sleeves accentuated the gracefulness of her arms. A narrow, braided belt resting low on her hips draped its length down her front, perfectly setting off the slimness of her waist. While she didn't attempt to tame her hair with veil, caul, or crespine, for the first time since they first met, she wore a shining circlet that came to point in the center of her forehead. Her simple, long braid, wrapped in ribbons the same blue as her gown, fell to her waist. With it being midsummer and warm, she had left off the sleeveless surcoat that might hide her mouthwatering curves. Valan reveled in the sight of her. A beauty, she was—nay, more than a mere beauty. Elspet was a goddess queen.

Her searching gaze settled on him, and she smiled, making his chest tighten even more. She was his. Forever and all time. He must remember to thank the Lady of Argyll whenever he saw her again. Lady Christiana had chosen well for him.

He hurried across the courtyard and took the wooden steps two at a time. This morning, when he forced himself to leave her bed, she had been asleep, all warm and tempting among the pillows. It had been all he could do not to stay with her. He greeted her with a kiss of her hand. "Ye are loveliness itself, m'lady. How fare ye this fine day?"

"I will be better when all is settled," she said under her breath. A furtive shifting of her eyes and a subtle jerk of her head warned him that Dullis or someone who might be a problem was near. Speaking louder, she continued, "I must admit, it feels quite strange to stand in the courtyard and hear nothing but the hopeful sounds of my people rebuilding their lives. The morning seems brighter with the siege ended."

"M'lady?" Dullis pulled the door open wider and joined them on the landing. "Since Himself arrives tomorrow, does there nay need to be a hunt for a fine venison to celebrate?"

"I am lady of this keep, and our beloved laird, *Himself*, sleeps inside his tomb." Elspet glowered at the woman. "Ye will refer to his brother as Master Euban. Not *Himself*. Do ye understand?"

Dullis's puckered scowl darkened even more. "Aye, m'lady. As ye wish." She gave a pointed glance down at the corner of the courtyard where smoke and the clattering of iron pots rose from the kitchens. "What do ye wish me to tell Cook about preparing for *Master* Euban?"

"Cook and her scullery folk will do as they have done since all from the village came to live within these walls. Prepare dinner enough for every man, woman, and child. If Euban wishes to eat, he can eat the same food his kin enjoy." Elspet stared the woman down, her tight-jawed glare daring the surly maid to challenge her.

Valan caught Dullis's attention with a fierce look of his own. He'd held his tongue as long as he could. "Do as yer mistress bids ye, aye? With *respect*, I might add."

Dullis jerked her chin downward, then disappeared back inside the hall.

"Walk with me to the battlements?" Elspet motioned toward the outer access stair to the rooftop of the gatehouse. She lowered her voice. "We should be safe to speak freely up there."

For the benefit of Dullis, who he felt certain still listened at the door, he gave a polite bow and offered his arm. Elspet accepted it with a graceful nod. But when they reached the middle landing of the outer stair, he brought them to a halt. In a low voice, he explained, "We should remain here, m'lady. Our *king's messenger* will arrive at any moment."

"As ye wish." Elspet's smile tensed as did her hold on his arm. "The order looks convincing enough?" She spoke without looking his way. Instead, she pointed at something across the courtyard as if they were discussing it.

"Better than I dared hope." He pointed at a different area close to the first imaginary object of their feigned interest.

"There is one thing that concerns me." She patted his arm as though agreeing with whatever he had said. "Why would the king send such an order about a distant cousin? How would he know that William was here or that he might wish to marry Beitris?"

Valan rested his hand atop hers and squeezed. He had thought of that as well. "Rest assured. We have that covered. William's mother and the king's mother are quite close. And in truth, William's mother never warmed to her son being a *Gallóglaigh*. To this day, his mother tracks him closer than a hound in chase of a scent and keeps herself apprised of his whereabouts and quests at all times."

"So, his mother whispered in Marie de Coucy's ear that a lairdship would grant her son a safer life than that of a mercenary?"

"Exactly."

Her grip on his arm relaxed. "Well done, fine sir. Well done, indeed."

A sudden horn blast from the southwest tower startled them both.

"Someone approaches." Elspet frowned at the tower as if wishing to silence it.

"Get inside."

"I will not." The indignation in her voice stopped Valan partway down the stair. "I never ran from the English. I willna run from whoever approaches."

"Elspet—"

"Nay, Valan. Now, leave off."

A spindly lad loped toward them, dodging chickens, geese, and milling townsfolk as he crossed the courtyard. "Lady Elspet! 'Tis Himself a comin'!"

"Euban Maxwell is not *Himself*." She hit the wood railing with her fist. "Ye will address him as Master Euban, ye ken?"

The youngling's face flushed red, and he backed up a step, bowing as he did so. "Aye, m'lady. Beg pardon."

She shooed the lad away with a flip of her hand. "Find Lady Beitris. Bring her to me. Make haste!"

The boy took off, running even faster than before.

"A day early." Elspet fisted both hands atop the railing. "'Tis just like him." Her gaze darted all over the courtyard.

Excitement hummed through the space. The people murmured and chatted as they gathered, craning their necks to see the man many of them thought should be their next laird.

Valan wished he had time to thrash some sense into them. Make them appreciate the woman who had given them her life. But there was no time. Instead, he took his place at her side and covered her trembling fist with his hand. "This is even better, my own. The bastard will witness the delivery of the king's message."

Her rapid breathing seemed to slow, but she still chewed on her bottom lip and didn't reply.

"Hold fast, m'love. Ye dinna face this bastard alone." Valan wished he could get word to Marcas and Roland but felt sure the two would know what to do when they saw Maxwell and his men approaching.

Lady Beitris, with William on her heels, emerged from the base of the southeast tower and ran across the courtyard. Valan noted that she, too, had set aside her armor and donned attire more befitting a laird's daughter. And she, like her mother, had not covered her coppery curls, but left them loose and streaming down her back. With both hands fisted in the dark green folds of her skirts, she held them up out of the way as she sped up the steps. Eyes wide, color high on her cheeks, she bared her teeth like a cornered animal. "Mama—he is nearly here."

Elspet wrapped an arm around her and hugged her close. "William and yerself are to act surprised by the order of marriage when it arrives. His mother and the king's mother have orchestrated it, not because the two of ye wish to marry, ye ken?"

Lady Beitris bobbed her head with a nervous jerk, then turned to William. "Understand?"

"Aye." William scowled at Valan. "Can we not just kill the

bastard and be done with all these games?"

"That is not the lady's wish." While Valan agreed with William, he trusted Elspet to know her people better than they did. So, it was best they do as she asked.

"Thank ye for seeking yet another escape from marrying me, William." Lady Beitris shot him a seething look.

The young warrior glared right back at her. "I would still marry ye, ye vicious wee hen. I canna imagine life without yer thorns in me arse. I've grown used to yer sting."

"Truly?" Lady Beitris's fiery facade melted, and she reached for him.

"None of that. Not yet." Elspet stepped between them. "Surprised. Do ye hear me?"

Both stepped apart with obedient nods.

The slow, steady clopping of horses echoed from the gatehouse tunnel as, single file, Euban and his men poured into the courtyard. At a glance, Valan reckoned at least a dozen. Maybe more. The interior of the castle strained to hold them. Valan assumed that the smug, barrel-chested man at the front was Euban.

Dressed all in black, dark hair and beard streaked with gray and disgusting in its greasy stringiness, the man dismounted, looking all around as if he already owned Caerlaverock.

Valan also noted the man kept smoothing down the hair on one side of his head with the regularity of a nervous twitch. He leaned toward Elspet. "Which ear did ye take?"

"The right," she said, confirming his suspicions. She pulled in a deep breath and eased it out. "I suppose we should properly greet him."

Valan stopped her. "Nay. Make him come to ye."

Elspet steadied herself at her post. "So be it, fine sir. Let our game begin."

CHAPTER SIX

W HEN EUBAN'S GLOATING smirk slid her way, it brought a surge of nauseating revulsion with it. Elspet forced herself not to shudder. She would not give the worm that satisfaction.

"Lady Elspet." He made a grand bow, then graced her with a victorious sneer. "It does my heart good to find Caerlaverock's portcullis raised and welcoming to us. Forgiveness is a grand thing for the soul, is it not?"

She stood taller and proudly lifted her chin, thankful for Valan's strength beside her. "Why have ye come, Master Euban?"

The man lifted both hands as if shocked she would ask. "Why, Lady Elspet—I have come to save my clan from the vile English. Sixty loyal men answer to my call. Hie yerself to the battlements and look to the south. They make camp now at the edge of the wood." Feigning a loud, despairing huff, he slowly shook his head. "We saw what was left of the village." His tone dripped with malicious taunting. "Was there naught ye could do against the English and their fiery brands?"

"The English have paid with their lives." She settled a proud gaze on Valan. "The Lord of Argyll was good enough to send his mighty *Gallóglaigh* to protect us." Determined to show him he would never rattle her, she cast a proud look across the village folk gathered in the courtyard. "Our clan will rebuild, and until then, they shall be safe and happy within Caerlaverock's walls.

There is room enough for all."

Euban ignored her. Instead, his leering focus slid to Beitris. He wet his lips, then made another courtly bow. "Lady Beitris, how can it be possible ye have grown even more lovely?"

"I have not," Beitris snapped. Her curled lip revealed how little she thought of him. "I hear as ye age, yer memory goes as well as yer eyes. Mayhap, that is yer problem."

Euban's toothy smile split his greasy beard. "Still a wee hell-cat in need of taming, I see." He scrubbed his hands together and licked his lips again. "I look forward to the task."

"Then ye look forward to death." Valan stepped forward. "These women are under my protection." He drew the short sword he carried sheathed beneath his arm. The blade caught the sunlight and reflected it in Euban's face. "Challenge me. I beg ye."

A low rumble rippled through the crowd. Whether because they were awestruck, dismayed, or rooting for the fight, Elspet couldn't tell.

"I am well within my rights here, mercenary dog." Euban swaggered forward, then made a sweeping gesture that encompassed the surroundings. "My brother left no son to follow him as laird. That honored title now falls to me. Even under the old law of Tanistry, I have been chosen as my brother's successor. Caerlaverock and Clan Maxwell are mine."

"Make way! Make way!" someone shouted from the opening of the gatehouse tunnel.

The crowd shifted, allowing an unremarkable man to pass. He carried a leather pouch strapped across his shoulder. A small mud-colored horse, as unmemorable as the man, plodded along behind him.

Elspet didn't recognize the messenger, but Valan had assured her that was why they had chosen Roland. She readied herself for the trickery about to play out. She could do this. Too many lives depended on the success of their ploy. As she leaned over the railing and peered closer at the man, Valan hissed something under his breath, but she didn't quite catch it. It didn't matter. She would act this out to convince Euban of the messenger's authenticity. Ready to be done with it, she hurried down the stair.

"Lady Elspet!"

She paused and looked back at him. Valan seemed more frustrated than she had ever seen him. "What is it?"

He shot a glare at the messenger, then looked back at her. Teeth clenched, he gave a subtle, jerking shake of his head.

Whatever troubled him had to wait. A private word was impossible now. She pushed onward.

The dusty traveler pulled a folded parchment from his pouch and held it high. "From His Royal Highness, King Alexander. Where be the laird of Clan Maxwell?"

"I am," Elspet and Euban replied in unison. Before Euban made it to the lad, Elspet shoved her way in front of him, wishing she had worn her armor instead of the infernal gown tangling around her ankles. Thank the saints they were in front of so many witnesses. Valan's messenger had timed this entrance well. "Here. Give it to me. I am Laird Herbert Maxwell's widow. The new laird is yet to be named."

The messenger held the sealed notice against his chest and backed up a step. "My king bade me give this to none other than the Maxwell himself."

"Laird Herbert Maxwell died months ago. In Wales. Fighting for King Alexander." She thrust out her hand and marched closer, ready to rip the thing from the man's clutches. Enough was enough. Time for the reveal. "Give it to me, and I shall read it for all to hear."

Before the man handed it over, Valan appeared at her side and caught hold of her arm. Something dark and frightening filled his eyes. His expression was dire. "M'lady," he said soft and low, then shook his head again in an adamant *no*.

"Let her be, *Gallóglaigh*," Euban growled as he shoved closer. A stench akin to rotting onions and stale piss accompanied him, wafting across everyone he neared.

Elspet turned aside to keep from gagging. The man always

had stunk worse than a ripe chamberpot. How could she have forgotten? She cast another worried glance at Valan. Something was wrong, and he was trying to warn her. But what could they do now? In front of the entire clan? And Euban? She held out her hand to the messenger again. "Give me the message. Now!"

Whether because of her tone or everyone closing in on him, the man shoved it into her hand, dipped a respectful nod, then hurried back through the gatehouse tunnel.

"What does it say?" Euban shoved closer, his hot, rancid breath hitting her full in the face.

She turned away, covering her mouth and nose with the back of her hand. "I shall read it aloud from the platform." As she passed Valan, he grabbed her arm.

"What do ye fear, *Gallóglaigh*?" Euban drawled. "Afraid the king has named me next laird because he discovered there are those who would dare challenge me?" His shoulders shook with his self-satisfied snickering. "In fact, I can almost guarantee ye that is what it says, since I came here straight from Kinghorn Castle where I paid my respects to His Majesty. I assured him I would be as loyal to him as my brother had been. Quite the important oath to the king, this being the borderlands and all."

A choking knot of bile burned in Elspet's throat. God help them all. Is that what Valan had been trying to tell her? She stumbled up the last step, barely catching herself before she fell across the landing.

"Mama!" Lady Beitris leapt to steady her, worry and confusion flashing in her eyes.

"I have failed ye, my daughter," Elspet whispered. "Please forgive me."

"Mama?"

"Open the damn message, woman." Euban swaggered forward, his repugnant stench clearing a path all around him. He smiled up at Elspet, then grabbed his crotch and wet his sausage-like lips again. "Ye best get used to doing as ye are told."

Valan lunged for the man and smashed his fist into his face.

"Valan!" Elspet cringed. The clan would surely rise against them. The courtyard already hummed with their rumblings.

Blood spurting from his nose, Euban clawed at Valan's hold on his throat. His men jumped on Valan to pull him away but made little progress, only succeeding in foiling his efforts to beat their master senseless.

"Mighty *Gallóglaigh*," William roared. "To arms!"

A wall of muscle surged forward. More of Euban's men poured in through the tunnel. Bystanders fled out of their path. Chaos ruled Caerlaverock, filling Elspet with shame. "To the tower, Beitris. Sound the horns to stop this madness."

Fisting her skirts out of the way, Beitris sped up the steps and into the hall to access the inner stair to the tower. A few moments later, the warning horn blew loud and long.

The brawling in the courtyard paused.

Elspet ripped her finger under the message's seal and waved it overhead. "Cease yer fighting and listen!"

With all eyes locked on her, she smoothed open the folds and stared down at the flowery script. Her blood turned to ice as the meaning of the wordy prose became clear. Euban Maxwell had spoken the truth. The parchment bearing the king's seal named him laird of Clan Maxwell to maintain peace among the clans and strengthen loyalties along the border.

She let it slip from her fingers and flutter to the ground. All was lost. There was naught she could do. Without a word, she turned and slowly climbed the stairs, coming to halt on the top landing. Euban would either order her and Beitris killed—or worse, keep them alive to torment. Head bowed, she prayed the vile dog would only send Valan and his men away and do them no harm. Her heart ached with the knowing that Valan wouldn't go. A tear slipped down her cheek. Nay, her mighty warrior would die trying to save her.

William's voice rang out, breaking through her fog of hopelessness as he read the order aloud. When he finished, silence filled the courtyard for a long moment before Euban's loud, arrogant clapping echoed off the walls.

"Did I not tell ye?" he crowed. "Lock up these traitorous mercenaries. Every last one of them. And the whore and her daughter, too. All of them failed to protect ye. I will not." Euban's men surged forward. Even more shoved into the courtyard.

Beitris joined her on the landing but was armed with her bow. Before Elspet could stop her, she let loose an arrow. It found its mark in Euban. He fell back, writhing and bellowing as several rushed to his aid.

"Beitris! He is laird by the king's order." Elspet snatched the bow from her and yanked the quiver off her back. "Do ye wish to be hanged for treason?"

"I dinna care," Beitris snapped. "He has no right."

"To the cages with them!" Euban bellowed, once more on his feet, his bloody hand clutching the arrow still in his shoulder. "Beat the insolence out of the bitches, then hang them from the northeast tower so they can count the sunrises as they wither and die."

"Feckin' thing didna fly true." Beitris tried to pull the bow from Elspet's hands. "Give it to me before they reach us!"

"Nay, my daughter." Elspet knocked an arrow and let it fly. "I shouldha done this years ago."

One of Euban's men shoved his master aside before the missile reached its mark. The arrow took that man down instead, burying deep in the base of his throat.

"Elspet!" Valan's roar rang in her ears as the men closed in on her and Beitris.

Rough hands grabbed and jerked. A hard cuff across her mouth filled it with the coppery taste of blood. A blinding blow to her eye made it ache and swell. She pulled her dagger from its hidden nest between her breasts and started slashing. She knew they would torture and kill her, but by all the angels in Heaven above, she would not go down without a fight and knew in her heart Beitris would fight them as well. What cut her to the quick was that some of those beating her were the very people she had served all her life. How had she wronged them so badly as to make them turn on her?

ELSPET HUGGED HERSELF against the constant onslaught of the whipping wind, taking care not to clutch her throbbing ribs too tightly. A deep breath was impossible. The pain nearly made her swoon. She squinted the eye not swollen shut in a vain attempt at focusing. Tears brought on by the stinging breeze blurred her vision. At least it was midsummer and warm. For now. Nightfall, rain, and the rough iron bars of her cramped prison would bring chilly hours until the sun returned. The chains securing the cages to the tower creaked and groaned above her. Their rancid, greasy coating occasionally dripped, hitting her with a dull splat. Directly below, the waters of the moat rippled, silently promising to drown her should the chains of her cage break.

"Feckin' bastards."

"Beitris…" Elspet clenched her teeth against the pain and shifted to face her, wishing their cages hung closer together so they might touch each other's hands.

Beitris's face was covered in reddish-purple bruising, her lip split and bleeding. But her fire remained. Her glaring scowl turned even more fierce. "Mama, they beat us. Stripped us down to our shifts. Trapped us in these feckin' cages dangling from the tower, and rain's coming. I dinna think the propriety of my language is a valid concern."

"True." Elspet repositioned herself again, impossibly hoping for a more comfortable spot. The height of the iron box prevented standing. Even sitting, the top of the cage forced her to hunch forward. "They are feckin' bastards, and I hope each of them burns in Hell."

"Valan and William will save us." Beitris peered down, spit, then flinched and touched her split lip. "Damn. I missed him."

"Ye have to account for the wind." Elspet swept her hair back from her face and spit.

"Ye missed, too."

"Aye. Not enough weight in spittle from this height."

"Ye didna agree with me about Valan and William saving us."

The suddenly solemn ring to Beitris's tone tugged at Elspet's heart. "They will save us if they can find a way." She couldn't bear to look at her daughter after that answer, remembering how Euban's men had swarmed in on every *Gallóglaigh* in the courtyard. "For the life of me, I dinna ken where Euban found so many to follow him."

"Englishmen, I'd wager. Feckin' traitor." Beitris swayed from side to side, making her cage swing until it banged against the wall.

"If ye make it fall, ye will drop straight into the moat and drown." Elspet shifted again and bunched up her shift under her rump. The iron slats, roughened until the edges were covered with nicks and burrs, dug into her bruised flesh.

"Do ye love him?"

"Who?"

"Ye know *who*." Beitris stopped swinging and shifted positions.

"I think I could. Verra much." Elspet leaned against the hard, cold bars and hugged her knees. "I hope he is not suffering because of us." The chains above her creaked as the cage slowly turned in the wind. "Do ye think ye might love William?"

"I think he is verra nice," Beitris said, sounding thoughtful. "They will save us if they can, aye?"

"Aye, dear daughter. They will save us if they can."

VALAN PACED BACK and forth across the filthy straw clinging to the stone floor. Captured. Disgust and shame made him snort. He hated the stench of failure. His invincible *Gallóglaigh* captured and jailed. Frustration lodged in his throat, threatening to choke him. Under his watch, his mighty men had fallen. What would his brothers say? They would say, *Move on. Dinna wallow in a failure. Make it right.*

He squinted up at the narrow opening that allowed the barest slit of daylight into the cell where they all awaited their fate. The thought of Elspet beaten, then trapped in a cage hanging from the tower drove him mad. At least it was summer. Hopefully, that guaranteed her survival until he could save her and Beitris.

"Sixteen of us." William kept his voice low while watching the door on the other side of the long, narrow room. "And not a single knave among us. At least they made it to the woods." The sixteen filled what had to be the only prison cell within Caerlaverock Castle. Located inside the gatehouse on the floor between the guards' barracks and the laird's private level, there wasn't room enough for another cell this size within the gaol.

"So, four *Gallóglaigh* and all the knaves remain free." Only twenty warriors and their knaves had come to Caerlaverock, not believing the protection of a castle this size to be that great a challenge. Valan ground his teeth until his jaws ached. Their pride had enabled Euman's men to take them down.

"At least there is hope, then." William leaned against the wall, glaring at the door as he crossed his arms over his chest. "'Tis a pity the king's messenger wasna intercepted and Roland set in his place."

"If Euban spoke the truth about his visit to Kinghorn Castle, he never wouldha believed our message." Valan continued pacing, scowling down at the floor as he walked. "I pray Elspet and Beitris survive until we save them." That troubled him most. Pride and reputation meant nothing if his precious Elspet died.

A deep belly laugh outside the door interrupted his tortured musing. He rushed to the wall beside it and prepared to attack whoever dared open it. William joined him. But the door remained shut. Valan turned his head to better hear the guards' conversation. They talked of feasting. Celebrating. One speaker caught his attention. He frowned at William and whispered, "Englishman?"

William slowly nodded, his eyes lighting with recognition. "During the attack, I knew I heard more than one bastard that didna sound like a Scot."

Valan brought a finger to his lips and pressed an ear to the door. More men arrived. Bottles clinked. Shouts and laughter rang out. Toasts of *Slàinte mhath!* and *To your health, mate!* filled the outer corridor. He motioned for his men to remain silent. With any luck, whatever spirits flowed so freely on the other side of that door would not only loose the tongues of Euban's men but also relax their guard.

"Ole King Edward'll surely make your laird one of the aristocracy, mate," one of the English voices said. "Prolly an earl or the like. Either way, he'll have a right good way of it what wif his siding with England."

"England?" A Scot guffawed. "'Pears to me old Maxwell's playin' both sides. King Alexander extended our clan's borders to the east and west. Heard the Maxwell say so m'self."

Valan locked eyes with William and read his own thoughts in the man's face. Euban Maxwell was not only a traitor to Scotland but England as well. The bastard intended to lend his loyalty to whichever side benefited him most, or both if he could get away with it.

"Orders, Constable?" hissed Gareth, one of their best archers.

"Orders, indeed." Valan eyed the door. "We canna ambush them when they bring us food because I dinna think that cruel bastard ordered us fed and watered. Nothing was brought last night, nor when the sun rose." He pushed away from the wall and moved closer to the tiny window too high on the outer wall to be of any use. Every man in the dank room watched him. "But then neither do I think he will leave us to rot, considering it be well into summer, and the stench would rise and join him in his chambers."

"Surely, he might try and torture us?" the grinning warrior known as Mathis suggested. "That door will have to open, then."

"Aye, but how long will he wait?" William asked. "Reckon he'll give it a while in an attempt to weaken us?"

"That thought had occurred to me." Valan returned to stand in front of the massive door and stared at it. Wide planks of oak reinforced with bands of iron. Unlike many prison doors, it contained no window or opening of any kind, and it was almost square rather than oblong. When the door was hung, the craftsmen left spaces at the top and bottom about four fingers wide. They could slide cups and bowls under the door, but he had no idea why the workmen had left that much space at the top. Poor design? Then it came to him, bringing him a victorious smile.

"Constable's got it now," said the mercenary known as Ruan from where he crouched in the corner. "Look at him."

Every man in the crude room of stone rose to their feet, ready for anything.

Valan motioned for all of them to draw closer to the back wall. He spoke in a hushed tone to keep his voice from traveling. "When night falls and the fine gentlemen on the other side of that door have celebrated their fill, we shall put our backs into it and lift that door off its hinges."

William jerked around as though startled by something behind him. He bent and patted the floor under the window high above their heads. "A message." He pulled a tiny piece of parchment out from a hollow reed and handed it to Valan.

Valan unrolled it and held it high, angling it to catch enough light to make out the cramped words. *Warned folk. Help sent. Help ladies when can. Please din leave me.* He peered closer and reread it.

"What's it say, m'lord?" Lachan, their best with a battle axe, squinted at the flowery writing. "That there's a woman's scrawl. Bet a groat on it."

"What's it say?" The whispered chant rippled through the men.

"Warned folk. Help sent. Help ladies when can. Please din leave me." Valan rolled the parchment back up and stuffed it into the reed. "How did ye ken a message was inside?" he asked William.

"The tip of it was sticking out the end of the reed."

"Good man." Spirits lifting, Valan swept aside the rancid straw against the wall with the toe of his boot, dropped the reed in place, then buried it. "In case our escape this evening fails. We must not betray our unknown messenger."

"Warned our folk," William repeated. "The ones of us not captured?"

"Them the only ones here that be our folk," Lachan said. "This be the tightest clan I have ever seen. Them there Maxwells dinna trust anyone not born into the clan."

"They proved that well enough by turning on Lady Elspet." Valan still couldn't believe her own people had chosen Euban over her. "Damned fools."

"And they sent for help," William said, then shook his head. "Take a few days to get to Argyll and back for more sword arms."

"Not with a man riding hard and trying to save his brethren." Valan rubbed a finger back and forth across his bottom lip as he repeated the words in his head. "But who could help the ladies whilst they're hanging in those cages?" He frowned up at the window. "It canna be Dullis. She's loyal to Euban."

"What about Lady Beitris's maid?" William asked.

"Never met her." He dimly recalled Elspet saying the woman's name was Fiona. "It nay matters who it is as long as they get food and water to our ladies when they can." That would buy them more time to escape by ensuring the survival of the women.

"Whoever it is doesna wish to stay here when we leave," William said.

"Because they fear Euban's wrath." Valan kicked more straw and dirt over the message, making certain it was buried deep. "We will take them with us when we leave, even though I dinna plan on leaving that worm alive."

"Perhaps we should," William suggested with a smug grin.

Valan stared at him, wondering if he had already gone mad from confinement. *"Perhaps we should?"*

"Aye." William winked and leaned back against the wall again. "I dinna believe our king takes kindly to those committing treason."

"True, but Maxwell's played up to Alexander. Gained his trust." He still preferred killing the bastard himself rather than allowing the king to have the pleasure of ending the traitor.

"Aye, but our connection to the king is stronger." William arched a brow, then winked again.

Valan agreed with a subtle nod, understanding that his second in command wished to keep his bloodline private. William wanted to be known as a warrior, not the cousin to the king. "I will consider leaving him alive."

He refused to make any promises. After all, he owed Euban a great debt. The man had tormented his lady love and destroyed her life's work. Valan flexed his fingers, itching to wrap them back around Maxwell's throat and squeeze.

A hard thump hit the cell door, followed by loud laughter.

Every warrior in the room grinned. Valan checked the window again, gauging the angle of the sunlight streaming in the tiny slot and hitting the floor. Several hours 'til nightfall and their best chance at freedom. He prayed they passed quickly. For Elspet's sake.

"I HEAR SNORING," Mathis whispered. On his hands and knees, he pressed his cheek against the floor and tried to peer underneath the door. "A lot of snoring. And by the looks of their feet, they couldna be more relaxed."

Valan motioned for him to stand. "Lachan, William, and I will lift the door. With the hinges on the outside, it should fall this way. When we back up, the rest of ye rush them. Drunk and dazed as they are, they should be easy enough to silence."

Several of the mercenaries cracked their knuckles. All nodded, their smiles bright in the room's dimness, lit only by the torchlight streaming in the openings at the top and bottom of the door. Every injury they had received during the ambush in the courtyard would now be repaid.

Valan chose the hinged side of the portal. William took the middle, and Lachan lumbered up and squatted on the side bearing the latch.

"What about the lock, m'lord?" Lachan whispered, pressing his eye snug against the crack of the door to see the mechanism.

"The door opens out," Valan said. "When they put us in here, I heard them drop the bar across it." He squatted down and took hold of the door's base. "Another reason why we must lift high as possible to undo the hinges then walk backward with it."

William crouched beside him and grabbed hold. Lachan set one large hand at the base of the door and rested the other up high to steady it once it came free.

"Together now." Valan locked his focus on the two men. "One...two...heave!"

They lifted the heavy barrier of oak and iron until the top of it hit the stones above. Straining to manage the cumbersome thing, Valan jerked his head for them to walk it back. At first, it gave, sending a rush of victory through his veins. But then it caught and refused to move any farther.

"Pull," he growled through clenched teeth.

The three of them, every muscle bulging, yanked. Something popped, then the sound of wood splintering gave them hope. "Pull," he groaned again.

"Escape!" shouted a guard. "Sound the alarm!"

The enemy's alarm gave them the strength they needed. The door came free so fast they stumbled back and nearly landed on their arses.

Valan slid free of the thing, holding it long enough to allow

William to get out from behind it. Lachan had already joined the others in silencing the guards.

A hard kick splintered the entrance to the armory. Valan rushed inside, searching for his belongings among the Maxwell's stores. He wanted his personal blades stained with the blood of those who had harmed his Elspet.

"Did any make it free to warn the rest?" he called out while sheathing extra daggers in both boots.

"None," William announced proudly. "Do we do this with stealth or loud bloodletting?"

"Stealth first. Until Elspet and Beitris are safe, ye ken?" Valan spotted several coiled ropes stored on pegs beside the spear rack. He grabbed them all, looped his arm through them, and shouldered them along with a mace bearing a handy leather strap. With a grim smile, he gave William a nod. "Spread the word. Once our ladies are safe, I grant each warrior free will to do his worst. Give no quarter."

William gave a delayed dip of his chin but stood fast, grimacing as if in pain.

Valan eyed the man, knowing what was running through his head. William fought well man to man, warrior to warrior. But with any takeover where innocents might get in the way, he always lagged back. "Harm no women or children, William. Ye ken that well enough. 'Tis a standing order. Always has been and still stands now. Ye should know that. I am not without a heart."

"And the aged or infirmed?"

Valan scrubbed a hand over his face. "How long have ye fought at my side?"

"Five years, m'lord."

"Have I ever ordered or allowed the massacre of anyone who could not defend themselves?" The young warrior's hesitation hurt as much as if one of his brothers had accused him of being a murderous barbarian. William did not know of the brutal deaths of his mother and sister and would not discover it now. But the man's attitude and doubts made him decide he had chosen the wrong *Gallóglaigh* as his second in command. "Answer me, Second. Have I ever ordered the murder of innocents?"

"Nay, m'lord." William dropped his gaze. "Forgive me." With a weak shrug, he added. "I feared that in yer rage, ye would kill everyone bearing the name of Maxwell."

"We waste precious time discussing this. Either help me save our ladies or see to the men. I dinna give a damn which ye choose. But know this, when this chore is done, ye will no longer be my second in command. Second in command doesna mean *second-guessing* my commands." Irritated at his own poor judge of character, Valan sheathed his sword and plowed around the man to get out the door. "Make my orders clear to the men," he added without looking back. Elspet mattered more than anything. He would deal with William later.

CHAPTER SEVEN

ROM THE SHADOWS at the base of the tower, Valan scanned the courtyard. Blazing torches beside the doorways sputtered, hissed, then finally extinguished in the torrential rain. The storm's murkiness dimmed the last two remaining beacons, the pair marking the entrance to the main banquet hall. Those lights would soon go out as well. Loud revelry from that side of the castle marked the feasting better than any flame. The noise along with the raging storm provided ample cover for the escaped warriors.

William appeared at his side. "The old guards in the gatehouse refused to leave their post, so we bound and gagged them. They tried to resist, but none of us had the heart to end them."

Valan remembered the two men. While William's decision to keep them alive pleased him, his second in command's earlier misgivings and lack of trust plagued him. In times of battle, trust made the difference between living and dying. Much needed to be cleared between them when this was over. He eased open the door to the tower stair and checked for anyone hiding within. Silence filled the dimly lit stairwell. Light from far too few torches made the winding way treacherous. He slipped inside, listened for a moment to ensure they were alone, then continued the conversation. "What of the remaining guard in the barracks?"

"Dead. Not a Maxwell guard remains in the gatehouse."

"And the outer camp? Euban's English forces?" With the

element of surprise on their side, his well-trained men, even though wounded and outnumbered, could scrub the camp of the sixty men Euban boasted to be his followers.

"Few were there," William said, staying close as they climbed the stone steps. "But those few are now dead."

"I am sure the rest are in the banquet hall." Valan charged up the last of the stairs, threw open the door, and emerged onto the rooftop. The dim light from a single brazier at its center did little to show him the way to the north tower. Driving rain and the blackness of the night fouled him even more. Arms outstretched, he squinted to find the battlement wall. Lightning flashed as if the gods decided to tease him with a fleeting glimpse of what lay ahead.

"Leave her be!" he bellowed up at the storm. He didn't care that it made him look foolish. He would fight every god in existence if that's what it took to save Elspet. A tug on the ropes looped over his shoulder made him turn.

"Tie off to me! More rope that way." William pointed father along the wall. "Lower the ropes to the cage and have them knot them around the bars. The chains are sure to be oiled. Too hard to pull up in this rain."

Valan doubted either woman possessed the strength to tie a knot strong enough to pull up the iron boxes, but William was right about one thing. Most who used such cages for torture knew to oil the chains to make an escape or rescue next to impossible. And the rain mixed with whatever grease or fat coated the metal would make the chore all the more difficult. He handed William one rope while he secured the other to the wall. A single cage might take more than one rope to lift it. No matter what it took, they would get the women to safety.

Lightning split the sky, blinding him. The cloying, metallic smell of its power tainted the rain. Thunder boomed so loud that the castle trembled. The storm was growing worse. They had to hurry. He leaned out over the battlement, wedging himself in the same crenel as the chain leading to one of the cages.

"Elspet!" he bellowed, trying to make himself heard over the storm. No answer. Fearful urgency pounded through him. A raw combination of anxiousness, rage, and dread made him lean farther out into the dark void. He barely made out a faint whiteness not too far below. It had to be one of the women. Something grabbed his belt, then thumped his back. He squinted back over his shoulder. William showed him the rope he had knotted around his own waist and waved for him to continue. Valan straightened and brought himself nose to nose with his second in command. "I have to climb down there. I canna make her hear me."

William hesitated for the span of a heartbeat, then gave a jerking nod. "I will feed out the rope so the stones dinna cut it." He untied it from his belt, moved it to the small of his back, and leaned back, positioning his hand on either side to keep it moving. "Wrap it round yer waist twice, then knot it."

Valan lashed it securely, hoisted himself over the wall, then slowly began his descent, using the cage's chain as a guide. Another flash of lightning illuminated the land, revealing poor Elspet balled up in an iron box barely big enough to hold a full-grown sheep. He ground his teeth and channeled his rage into descending faster. Euban Maxwell would pay for this. By all that was holy, he would pay.

His footing slipped. Beneath summer's damp warmth, the sandstone blocks of the tower had sprouted patches of treacherous moss. His hands became raw from the bite of the rope. Ignoring the pain, he eased himself lower. He reached an iron bar at the end of the main chain. It was the yoke that held two chains attached to the sides of the crate.

"Elspet!" he shouted, willing her to hear him over the wind and rain.

The glimmer of white moved. She raised up and stretched her arm through the bars of the cage, reaching for him. Another flash of lightning revealed the terror in her face. "Valan!"

He drew up even with the top of her cruel prison, feeling all around the edges, searching for the latch. There was no need for a lock. The greased chains prevented any climbing out to escape. Lightning exploded too close. Deafening thunder followed.

Elspet fell back and balled up, covering her head with her hands.

"God guide me." He bowed his head and concentrated. His fingers finally found what had to be the latch. A joyous roar escaped him as he undid the simple metal catch and opened the lid. "Elspet! Come to me, my own!"

She paused but for a second, then stood, swaying to her full height as she grappled for him.

He swung closer and clutched her to his chest. "Hold tight, m'love. Hold tight."

She didn't answer, just wrapped her arms and legs around him.

Little by little, drawing on every ounce of strength he possessed, they inched upward. He prayed she had the strength to hold fast, because he needed both hands to climb. He daren't trust the treacherous slickness of the tower walls. The rope vibrated in his hold and started pulling him up, seemingly of its own accord. William. They had finally gotten close enough for William to see them making progress. He wrapped an arm around Elspet and hugged her close while holding the rope with the other hand and doing his best to walk up the wall.

When they reached the top, William took hold of her and lifted her to safety. Still hanging over the wall, Valan sagged against it, thanking the Almighty for saving Elspet's life.

"Constable! Take my hand!"

Valan grabbed hold and climbed over the battlement. He fell to his knees beside his precious lady and gathered her to his chest. "Thank God," he rasped, tilting her face up to his. "I feared…I feared…" He couldn't say the words aloud, but oh by God above, how he had feared he wouldn't reach her in time.

When she reached to caress him, bringing her fingers close enough to see, his rage flared hotter.

Her graceful hands were cut and oozing blood. Her nails were ragged and broken. "They took Beitris," she croaked, her voice spent from screaming. "They took her right before nightfall."

"Who?" Although he already knew without hearing her answer. "William!" he bellowed, twisting to search the area for the young warrior.

William stood a short distance away, Beitris's empty cage clutched between his hands. Eyes wild, he threw it against the wall. "Where is she?"

Lightning speared down in great, jagged spikes. Thunder rolled like boulders loosed upon the earth, ending in a deafening boom. It was as though the storm kept pace with William's bloodlust.

Valan waved the enraged warrior closer.

William crouched beside them and leaned in, squinting against another strike of lightning.

"She said they took her," Valan shouted as thunder followed. "Just before nightfall."

"Euban has always lusted for Beitris," Elspet cried out, blinking against the rain pelting her face. "Kill him." She reached for William. When he leaned toward her, she knotted his tunic in her fist and shook it. "If ye ever felt anything for her, kill him and save her."

"He will die," William swore, the fury in his eyes raging harder than the storm. "It willna be quick, neither will it be merciful."

"The cage for him, William." Valan jerked his chin toward the battlement. "What say ye?"

"Aye." William stood, unsheathed his sword, and pulled a battle axe free of the leather strapping he had crisscrossed between his shoulders. "Let us join Laird Maxwell's celebration and invite him outside for a bit of air."

Valan scooped Elspet up and held her close as he ran across the rooftop to the tower door. Once inside, he paused and leaned back against the wall. "I will take ye to the stable to hide while William and I find Beitris and settle with Euban."

"I pray he hasna harmed her." She lifted a trembling hand to her eye that was swelled shut. "I shouldha killed the bastard when I had the chance."

"We shall tend to that chore gladly, m'lady." He gentled a kiss to her temple, then turned his attention to William. "Gather the men whilst I take Elspet to safety."

Jaw set in a hard line, William gave a jerking nod, then bolted down the steps.

Valan started down the staircase, carefully feeling for each step.

She sagged against him, nestling her face in the crook of his neck. "I knew ye would come," she whispered.

"None of this shouldha ever happened." He almost choked on the all-consuming rage. "Forgive me, dear one. I beg ye."

She brushed a tender kiss to his throat and flattened her hand against his chest. "There is nothing to forgive, m'love. Nothing at all."

Her battered state concerned him, but he knew her love for Beitris would strengthen her. Once inside the stable, warm, dry, and hidden in a back stall, she could rest until all was made right again.

Keeping to the shadows, he crossed the courtyard and slipped into the small area connected to the small forge the smithy used for smaller projects and shoeing animals. The place was deserted, but heat from the red, glowing coals filled the space. Valan chose the darkest corner loaded with clean straw. He eased her down into it, fetched the smithy's heavy leather apron off the peg beside the forge, and draped it across her.

"Lovely warmth," she whispered, smiling as she snuggled down into it.

"It pains me to leave ye." He smoothed her wet hair back from her face, his hand lingering to touch her clammy cheek.

"It pains me to be so weak that I canna save my own daughter and kill Euban myself." She covered his hand with hers and held it. "I know ye willna fail. That alone enables me to rest here and wait."

"I love ye, Elspet." Again, as when he had asked her to marry him, the words sprang from him unbidden. But this time they didn't shock him. Nay. This time he knew his heart had taken control, saying that which needed to be said. "I love ye, my own," he whispered again, then pressed a kiss to her forehead.

"And I love ye, as well, my fine warrior." She touched his face, smoothing her thumb across a swollen line along his cheekbone. "Come back to me safely, aye?"

"I will," he promised. "With Beitris on my arm." He pulled a dagger from his boot and pressed it into her hands. "I willna fail ye, but I willna leave ye without a weapon, either."

She hugged it to her chest, her eyes filling with more tears. "I shall pray both of ye safe and returned to me with haste."

"I must go now." He forced himself to stand and step away even though he loathed leaving her. With a last look around to ensure no danger lurked in the shadows, he slipped out into the courtyard. A subtle movement in the darkness beneath the eaves of the buildings across the way halted him. He pressed his back against the wall and remained motionless until he heard a low growl from a dog that wasn't there. A different growl followed. Then after a moment or so, a yipping bark. The animal sounds were one of the many ways his warriors communicated when the situation warranted. Each of them now knew all had gathered. The time to attack was at hand.

He sprinted across the courtyard and joined the eight or so men creeping along the wall to the left of the banquet hall entrance. The rest of his warriors eased along the wall to the right. The noise inside had swelled to a loud, raucous pitch. Dangerously so. It was the sound of evil at work. Valan readied his sword and axe and gave Gareth the signal to follow with an arrow nocked in his bow. "Dinna kill the bastard," he warned. "We wish to give Euban Maxwell a lovely lingering death in the cages."

Gareth grinned and agreed with a single nod.

They slipped into the room. Not a single reveler noticed. Savage fury consumed Valan when he turned and saw why.

At the head of the room, on her back across the main table with her wrists and ankles bound to its legs, Beitris lay naked and sobbing.

Euban hovered over her, dribbling wine down between her breasts and her stomach, then bending to lick it up.

Valan ordered the attack with a downward slash of his sword.

Gareth's aim was true as always.

The arrow split Euban's outstretched tongue before it reached Beitris's pale flesh. He roared and clutched at his mouth, stumbling backward off the pedestal. The hall erupted into drunken chaos. The sixteen *Gallóglaigh* swarmed.

Sword and axe stained red, Valan slashed his way to the front of the room, rounded the dais, and bore down on Euban. Instead of finishing the man with a humane slash of his sword, he dragged him over to the wide oak beam of the archway. With dead aim, he drove his dagger through Euban's palm, nailing the bastard to the wood.

Unable to speak. Blood streaming down his front. Euban's gurgling turned to hysterical shrieks as Valan thrust another dagger through his arm, pinning it to the timber, too. Satisfied for the moment, he ripped a tapestry off the wall and threw it across Beitris before cutting her arms and legs free.

"Give me a blade!" She clutched the weave around herself and rolled off the table.

Valan held out a dagger, but when she went to take it, he refused to let go until she understood. "Dinna kill the devil, m'lady. William has the cage waiting for him. He doesna deserve a quick death." By the subtle shifting of the wildness in her eyes, he knew she agreed. He released his hold on the knife and stepped back.

One hand clutching the wrap to her chest, she slowly made

her way to where Euban sobbed and writhed in pain. She cut through his belt, sliced away his trews, then lifted his bollocks with the blade.

Euban shrieked louder and tried to kick her away, but each time he lifted a foot, she stabbed his thighs. "Mama took yer ear. I willna take anything from ye, but I will feed ye yer bollocks!" She sliced them off, skewered them with the tip of the knife, and shoved them into his mouth. Then she backed away, chest heaving and eyes glittering with fury.

"Well done, Lady Beitris." Valan admired the woman. Even though cruelly abused and humiliated, she had found the strength to fight back. Her courage to be a survivor rather than a victim humbled him. She was the mightiest of warriors.

As the din settled, Valan turned, searching for his men. Blood covered every surface. Bodies sagged across tables, sprawled across the floor, and slumped over benches. But not a single one belonged to his mighty *Gallóglaigh*. Pride and a sense of justice made him stand taller. He settled a pointed gaze on William, then shifted it to Beitris, where she raged back and forth in front of the unconscious Euban, mumbling under her breath.

William understood Valan's unspoken message. He went to her with empty hands lifted and held them out to her. When he came within a single stride of her, she raised her dagger as though ready to charge and attack. He stood still. Both hands still raised, waiting without saying a word.

The crazed look in her eyes faded, and the blade dropped from her hand. She staggered forward and almost fell to her knees. William grabbed her up and held her. Eyes closed, he cradled her with a gentleness that betrayed his true feelings. She curled into his chest and filled the hall with her loud, keening sobs.

The siege successful, Valan scrubbed a weary hand across his face. Time now to heal and help his lady rebuild her life.

ELSPET STARED OUT the window as Fiona, Beitris's faithful maid, combed her freshly washed hair with gentle, careful strokes. "See to Lady Beitris, Fiona. I can manage my dressing. Truly, I can."

With an understanding nod, Fiona returned the comb to the dressing table. Made of carved ivory, it had been a long-ago gift from Herbert. Elspet turned and stared at it where it lay among her things. 'Twas a wonder her departed husband hadn't risen from the tomb to save his daughter from the unspeakable acts committed by his own brother.

The elderly maid shuffled closer and cleared her throat with a hesitant *harrumph*. When Elspet looked her way, Fiona's hopeful smile plumped her withered cheeks and deepened the wrinkles around her kind eyes. "Our wee lamb is strong as they come, m'lady."

"That she is." Elspet reached out and took hold of the caring matron's knobby hands. "I am indebted to ye, Fiona. Ye risked yer life bringing us water while we were in those cages."

The dear woman's blue eyes filled with unshed tears. "I been nurse to Lady Beitris since her birth and served yerself many a year afore the Maxwell brought in Dullis. I couldna kill that bastard Euban for ye or get ye free, but I could bring ye water."

"Yer loyalty and bravery mean more to me than ye will ever understand." She squeezed the maid's hands again. "Ye will always have a place with us, Fiona. Always."

With a hitching sniff, Fiona bobbed her head. "I shall see to the Lady Beitris now. 'Tis my hope she's asleep since her bath and the warm whisky I fixed for her. The salve helped her bruises, too. I know ye will be pleased to see her so improved, m'lady."

"Send for me if anything goes awry, ye ken?" Beitris's courage made Elspet proud but frustrated her, too. The stubborn lass had waved her aside, claiming a woman grown didn't need fussing over by her mother. Especially when her mother had been beaten, too. Fiona was her only hope of keeping a watchful eye on her independent daughter. She trusted no one else in Caerlaverock.

Valan had told her what the bastard did, and how the rest had stood by and watched. The soulless devil now hung in his own cage, waiting to die. The others she would deal with later. After she'd rested enough to sort through her jumbled mind.

Fiona gently cleared her throat as she eased her hands free of Elspet's grasp.

"Forgive me, Fiona. I have so much on my mind." She peered intently at her, willing the dear old soul to understand. "Please, if my Beitris is sleeping, bring word, so I know she rests. I worry for her, but she wishes to be left alone."

Fiona fished a square of linen out of her apron pocket and dabbed it to the corners of her eyes. "I will, m'lady. Have no fear. I shall bring ye word of our wee lamb." She dipped a hurried curtsy and scuttled out the door.

Elspet steadied herself against the window ledge, watching Valan's men tear down the deserted encampment of Euban's followers. Whatever they recovered from the tents could be divvied out amongst the villagers. Or burned. The longer she watched, the more she realized she no longer cared about the clan or what became of them. They had beaten that out of her. And yet, because of that lack of caring, she felt a disturbing guilt she knew she didn't deserve. She kept telling herself to cast the unearned remorse aside but couldn't find a way how.

A light tapping on the door made her turn. "Aye?"

The door eased open, and Valan stepped across the threshold and then came to a halt. "I had to see ye."

Such a simple thing for him to say, yet it filled her with such joy. The deep rasping of his caring tone gave her a peacefulness she sorely needed. Hands outstretched, she started toward him. He met her halfway, pulling her into a gentle embrace that she never wanted to leave. "I am glad ye needed to see me," she said, pressing her forehead to the warmth of his throat. "I feel—" So much churned in her heart, she couldn't put it into words. Being safe at last. Lonely no more. Loved. Cherished. None of those words came close to describing the emotions coursing through her. "I feel so—" Overwhelmed, she gave up trying to speak.

"I, as well." He stroked her hair and held her closer. "I feared…"

She smiled as he went silent, unable to utter the words. "I know." Sudden lightheadedness made her clutch him tighter.

"Elspet?"

"Perhaps we should sit. I havena eaten yet. Fiona wished it, but the soothing the bath promised me was too tempting to resist."

He swept her up into his arms, carried her to the bed, and laid her gently among the pillows. Worry and concern creased his brow as he settled beside her. "Is she fetching food for ye now?"

Elspet sank back into the pillows, thankful for their softness against the bruises and cuts covering her back. "She will bring it after she checks on Beitris for me. I need her to do that more than I need bread."

His jaw tightened, flexing the muscles in his cheeks. "How is the Lady Beitris?"

"Almost too good." Elspet feared for her daughter. Dark memories could be sly, dangerous things, striking when least expected if not dealt with head-on. "She has always been strong, but I fear this will test her more than she can bear."

He lifted her hand, kissed it, then held it between both of his. "We will do whatever is needed to help her." Her uncontrollable shivering made him pull a coverlet from the foot of the bed and spread it across her. "I set the servants to scrubbing the hall and bleaching it with lye." His look of caring concern turned into a dark scowl. "We have yet to locate Dullis. If she is hiding to do ye harm—"

Elspet lifted a hand and stopped him. "I am sure she ran when she realized Euban's cause was lost. Probably returned to her kin farther north."

"For her sake, that would be wise."

His gaze dropped to their clasped hands. He idly rubbed his calloused thumb back and forth across her bruised knuckles, but she welcomed the sensation. It meant she was with him. But something else bothered him. She felt it just as surely as she felt his hand holding hers.

"Only truth between us," she gently reminded. "What troubles ye, my fine warrior?"

"While the rest of us were imprisoned, Artan sent for help." He pecked another quick kiss to her wrist. "I guarantee ye that Niall, my knave, rode like the hounds of Hell had been loosed upon him." He lifted his head and looked her in the eyes. "My clan will answer the call and be here within days."

"At least yer clan is loyal to ye." She made no attempt to hide her bitterness. Nay. Clan Maxwell, those she had cared for and served all her life, had turned their backs on her and Beitris when they needed them most. She blamed them as well as Euban for every atrocity carried out. With a hard swallow, she forced the burning betrayal aside and struggled to focus on whatever troubled Valan. "Yer clan is welcome to anything and everything here at Caerlaverock. Why does their arrival worry ye?"

"They will want to know what ye wish done."

"What I wish done?"

"Not all of Euban's more active followers died by our blades, nor did they run. They are in yer prison awaiting yer judgment." His chin lifted to a determined angle. "And then there are those who did nothing to save ye. Went along with the bastard in silence. Cowering in the shadows to save themselves. In my opinion, they deserve to be judged as well." He eased forward, a fierceness flashing in his eyes. "What do ye wish done with this clan, m'love? With Caerlaverock? I know ye once thought this place Beitris's right, but do ye truly think that way still? After all that has happened?"

Elspet stared at him, trying to sort through her jumbled thoughts and emotions as she sought refuge in his gaze. The angry red scrapes and purplish swellings on his face and arms made her breathing hitch. How could she explain what she wanted to be done, and how she felt about this place when she didn't know for certain herself? Best to start with the cold, dead weight that settled in her chest whenever she thought about those who had once been her people. "I dinna care what happens to this place or the land. All I care about is a life at yer side." There. She had said aloud the thoughts that filled her with a sense of shame she knew she didn't deserve.

He didn't respond, just shifted on the edge of the bed, and stared back down at their clasped hands. "I ken well enough ye feel that way now." He lifted his head and smiled. "And am thankful for it more than ye know." With a soft squeeze of her hand, he continued. "But ye may not feel that way in a few days' time. Ye may wish to help Lady Beitris rebuild and rule here."

"My daughter wishes this castle razed to the ground until naught remains to remind anyone of its existence." Beitris had uttered those very words while bathing. The poor lamb had scrubbed her skin so raw, she bled. Fiona had to snatch the rag away to keep her from harming herself further. "We can allow her time to see if her feelings change, but I verra much doubt they will. The stench of betrayal canna be scrubbed away with lye."

A knock on the door stopped her from saying any more. Before she could call out and bid them enter, Valan hurried to answer it. He opened it the barest bit, then nodded and stepped back to grant Fiona entry. His protectiveness made her smile.

"Ye brought her plenty to eat?" He trailed along beside Fiona, lifting the cloth covering the tray and scowling at whatever hid beneath it.

"Aye, m'lord." Fiona offered him a cheery smile before turning her happiness on Elspet. "And Lady Beitris is fast asleep. Peaceful as if cradled by the angels." Her rosy cheeks reddened even more as she cast a shy glance at Valan. "And Master William is sitting outside her door. Guarding her. No one passes if they dinna have a reason that suits him."

Elspet pushed herself higher in the bed, more than a little pleased with Fiona's report. "I am glad." She nodded at Valan as she sipped what appeared to be mulled wine but turned out to be a fruity broth instead. "I have always liked William. Perhaps he has changed his thinking about marriage after all." But then she remembered the match between Beitris and William no longer mattered. A heavy sigh escaped her. What would Beitris wish to do now?

"Their marriage, m'lady?" Fiona cocked a sparse brow as she plumped the pillows and adjusted the covers. When Elspet didn't answer, she aimed an inquisitive look at Valan.

"It matters not," Elspet said quietly, staring down at the thick slice of buttered bread and sliced apples in front of her. But if Beitris decided not to marry William, would she be content to live somewhere else and start life anew? Would she be inclined to live with Valan and herself—wherever that might be? Elspet studied him, her fretting spinning into worry. Would he be willing to accept the responsibilities of a grown daughter?

"Shall I bring ye something, m'lord? Food? Drink?" Ready to run as soon as he gave the order, Fiona wiped her hands on her apron.

He shook his head while keeping an uncomfortably watchful gaze locked on Elspet. "Nothing, thank ye."

"Verra well then." The maid bustled to the door and paused halfway across the threshold. "I shall be along later to collect the tray and check on ye. Rest ye well, m'lady. Send for me if ye need me sooner, aye?"

"Thank ye, Fiona." Elspet pinched off a bit of crust and tried to eat, knowing if she didn't, Valan would fuss.

"Nothing but truth between us, m'lady. Remember?" He nodded at her food. "Eat, m'love, and tell me yer worries so I might lay them to rest."

She rested her hands on either side of her plate. "For the first time in my life, I dinna ken what would be the best course of action. For Beitris or I." Massaging her temples, she closed her good eye, at war with so many conflicting possibilities.

His silence caused her to open her eye and find him watching her. Waiting.

"All I know for certain is I wish for us to be together." She pushed a slice of apple around the edge of the plate. "But I dinna ken what that means, either. For us. For Beitris." In spite of herself, tears welled and then escaped down her cheeks.

"Dear one," Valan said so softly it made her cry harder. He moved the tray to the table beside the bed, then settled back beside her, and eased her into his arms. "Nothing must be decided today. I should nay have troubled ye with anything until ye've fully rested and healed." He cradled her closer and settled his cheek to the top of her head. "Forgive me," he whispered. "All that matters now is ye are safe, Beitris is safe, and all of us are together, ye ken?"

"I no longer trust any of them," she whispered. "Nor do I care what befalls them." But her conscience pricked her. "Does that make me as manipulative and evil as Euban?"

"Ye could never be evil. Or manipulative." He shifted, kissed the top her head, then rested his cheek back on it. "Ye've nay got it within ye to do so." He idly fiddled with the lacy edge of her sleeve, straightening it along her wrist. "They betrayed ye and lost yer trust when they allowed ye tortured and Beitris ravaged. 'Tis only natural ye're ready to toss them to the winds of chance." With as little shaking of the bed as possible, he kicked off his boots and stretched out his legs across the bed. "Sleep now, aye?" He pulled the covers higher around her shoulders and kissed her forehead. "I am right here, and here I will stay. Holding ye. Keeping ye safe. Close yer eyes, my weary one. We've plenty of time to decide the best course for our lives."

"I love ye," she whispered, sinking deeper into the warm, safe darkness of his embrace.

"I love ye, too, my courageous queen. I love ye, too."

CHAPTER EIGHT

V ALAN KNEW THEY would come.

Brothers by blood as well as by blade. Nothing spurred them to action like one of their brethren in need. Thorburn, his eldest sibling, led the thunderous army galloping toward them. The sight of Ross, his middle brother, riding close to Thorburn, tightened his chest. When last he visited Tòrrelise, Ross had been so weak from a month's long illness, he had struggled to sit outside his keep in the sunshine. And yet here he was, riding as tall and strong as ever.

"So many." Elspet stood beside him. She tucked her arm through his and drew closer. Today was the first time she had conquered her demons and visited the battlement atop the gatehouse. The place where she and Beitris had received the worst of their beatings before being shoved into the cages. "Is that the entirety of yer clan?"

"Nay, m'lady. 'Tis but a small portion of the Lord of Argyll's mighty *Gallóglaigh*." He pointed at the front of the mass bearing down upon them from the north. "The two leaders there, those are my brothers. Thorburn at the left and Ross to the right, almost even with him." He couldn't resist a grin. "I grant ye before they reach us, Ross will try to overtake him because he knows how much Thorburn hates it."

"Viking blood runs strong in the three of ye," she said. "Fair-haired. Massive. Muscular." A pensive air surrounded her. "Pity

Euban didna live long enough to see this coming at him."

"True." Valan sidled a glance to the right and allowed himself a subtle, satisfied nod. Euban's body and all signs of the cages had been cleared away. Even the stone wall had been scrubbed to remove any stains of what had taken place at the northeast tower. He gave her arm a gentle pat and turned them toward the stair. "Come. Let us go below and greet them, aye?"

She lifted her chin as if readying herself for a difficult chore. "Aye. I wish them to know how grateful I am for their haste in coming here." After a hesitant twitch of her shoulders, she added, "Had ye not escaped and overcome those fiends, their arrival would have saved us for certain." After a tensed moment, a soft groan, like the whine of a frightened pup, escaped her.

"Only the truth, m'lady." He opened the door of the northwest tower leading to the stairs. "Tell me, dear one. Before we go down and meet them."

Her mouth tightened into a troubled line, then relaxed. Without answering, she stepped forward, making Valan wonder if she would share whatever troubled her so. As they started down the twisting staircase, she trailed a hand along the wall, her fingers trembling the barest bit. Finally, she spoke. "I must make my choice now that yer kin have arrived. They will need to know what Beitris and I wish done with those in our prison—as well as everything else."

Over the past few days, while she healed and recovered from all that had happened, he hadn't pressed her, even though he sorely wanted to know what she had decided. "The matter of William and Beitris is settled at least."

That earned a soft laugh from her. "God help that brave young man." Her steps slowed, and she looked up at him with a genuinely pleased smile. "If my grandchildren inherit their parents' red hair along with their fire and stubbornness, life will be interesting indeed."

"Have they said if they wish to remain here and rebuild the clan?" William had refused to tell him anything. A noble stance, but also so frustrating, Valan wanted to thrash his arse for him.

"They have not chosen Caerlaverock." Elspet halted. She stared down at the steps, a frown puckering her brow. "Beitris tells me William wishes to return to Argyll. She even said she looks forward to seeing that part of Scotland." With the barest shake of her head, she trembled with a faint shrug. "She's never been away from Maxwell lands before. Not ever." Her troubled gaze slid from the stairwell to him. "She wants no part of this place ever again. While her father brought nothing but honor to Clan Maxwell, she says the treasonous acts committed by Euban and his ilk have left a stain that canna be removed." Her frown deepened. "It appears the chore of rebuilding Clan Maxwell's honor, as well as the village, falls to me."

While Valan didn't wish to reside in the borderlands, if Elspet chose to do so, then so be it. He would stay at her side. A life with her was more than worth it. He brushed a kiss to her cheek. "Know that whatever ye choose, I am with ye, m'lady. Always."

Even in the dimness of the stairwell, the sheen of unshed tears made her eyes glisten. She reached up and touched his cheek. "And for that, I am more grateful than ye will ever know."

He lowered his mouth to hers, fueling the kiss with tender reassurance.

Her hands slid up his chest, then her arms hugged around his neck. She molded against him, her softness perfectly fitting his hardness. It made him entertain thoughts of taking her up against the wall, but the possibility of slipping on the narrow stone steps and tumbling down them brought him to his senses.

As much as he hated to break their connection, he lifted his head and groaned. "Come. I want my brothers to meet my future wife."

"And here I thought to delay the inevitable," she teased with a disappointed laugh.

"We will return to where we left off as soon as possible, m'lady. I assure ye." He placed her hand back in the crook of his arm, enjoying the swell of her breast rubbing against him with every step. Aye, they would most definitely pick up right where they had left off at their earliest possible opportunity.

They exited the tower and gatehouse and waited at the end of the bridge across the moat. The army of *Gallóglaigh* slowed, then fanned out, filling the grassy lands surrounding the castle.

Valan strode forward to meet them, greeting them with a hearty wave and hand signal they would recognize. "All is well," he bellowed. "Welcome!"

Thorburn lifted a hand and glanced all around, a signal to his men. The warriors behind him halted their mounts and remained in their saddles. All except Ross. He rode forward with his brother and dismounted.

"I told ye we would get here and discover the pup just fine and having no need for us." Ross shot a lopsided grin at Thorburn.

"And glad I am of it." Thorburn dismounted, swaggered forward, and grabbed Valan into a burly brother hug. "Ye scared the shite out of me," he said in a gruff whisper, then thumped his back. Grabbing hold of his shoulders, he gave him a hard shake. "Dinna do that again, young one. Understand?"

Before Valan could answer, Ross grabbed him next, shook him even harder, then lowered a stern scowl on him. "Did I not say ye would be a fine constable?"

"That ye did, brother." Valan's chest swelled with the rare praise. The MacDougall brothers were each other's harshest critics. "Come. I have someone I wish ye to meet."

"Damn. We should never have argued with Adellis and Elise," Thorburn said to Ross.

Ross gave a heavy sigh. "Aye, brother. It appears we have lost the bet."

Valan came to a halt before they reached Elspet. He lowered his voice so she wouldn't hear. "What bet?"

"Both Adellis and Elise said Lady Christiana had found ye a proper match, and *that* was why our liege insisted ye lead the campaign here at Caerlaverock." Thorburn raised both hands in the air. "After all, he couldha just as easily sent one of us or our seconds." He jutted his bearded chin to a challenging angle. "What say ye to that? Has the matchmaker succeeded?"

Valan stepped forward and curled an arm around Elspet. "I say, this be the Lady Elspet Maxwell, my future bride."

Elspet charmed them with a winning smile, just as he had known she would. "Welcome to Caerlaverock, m'lords, and please dinna think yer trip wasted." She paused, her full lips quivering just a bit. "If Valan and his men hadna been able to outwit their captors, ye would have been sorely needed for certain."

Thorburn smiled and granted her a polite bow. "Praise be that Valan and his men reigned supreme and overcame the traitorous fiends."

"By the way," Ross interjected. "Did ye ken that William's mother is kin to Marie de Coucy—the king's mother?" His upper lip curled as if dreading something dire. "Pray tell us the boy is alive and well. If not, it will be all our arses."

"Alive, well, and betrothed to my daughter," Elspet said with an amused tip of her head. She turned to lead the way inside the castle, then paused and glanced back. "Caerlaverock canna hold all yer men, but as many as can fit are welcome to come inside and sup with us."

"Our men will make camp out here, m'lady," Thorburn said. He cast a glance at the scorched plain where the village once stood. "Niall warned us there is much rebuilding to be done. Since we appear to be unneeded for battle, perhaps we can help with that." His focus shifted to Valan. "Or at least get it started. It was not our intent to be here long. Merely long enough to make things right, then return to our duties in Argyll." The intensity of his stare hardened. "Will ye be returning with us, Valan? Or are ye now the new master of this keep?"

Valan turned to Elspet. "How shall I answer that, m'lady?"

She settled what appeared to be a longing glance on Caerlaverock, then let her gaze drop to the ground. After what seemed like forever, she lifted her head, pulled in a deep breath, and blew it out. "This place is no longer my home," she said. "Or my responsibility." She managed a smile that didn't reach her eyes. "A prison full of traitors, a hall stained with my daughter's blood, and a tower haunted with demons. I shake the dust of this place from my shoes and willna look back at it when we leave." She turned to Thorburn and squared her shoulders. "Do as ye wish about helping them rebuild. In my opinion, 'tis high time they learned to help themselves. Perhaps that will make them realize what sort of person their next leader should be."

Thorburn's eyes narrowed. He pursed his lips and gave a slow nod. He met eyes with Ross, and the two brothers appeared to exchange a silent communication.

Valan understood completely. While he didn't know for certain what passed between them, he had a fair idea.

Ross confirmed it with another polite bow. "The two of ye are welcome to stay with me and my family at Tòrrelise until renovations are finished at Creagshead."

"Renovations?" Valan went to Elspet, wrapped an arm around her, and pulled her closer, glad of the decision she had found the strength to make but confused at his brother's announcement. "Who ordered renovations on my land?"

Ross and Thorburn shared a mischievous wink, then turned to him with proud smiles. "Lady Christiana. She felt certain ye would need the place made fit to live in. Appears she knew ye'd neglected the whole of it except the one bedchamber over the past five years."

Elspet gave him a confused frown. "Why would ye let the rest fall into ruin?"

Valan shook his head. "I needed naught but the bedchamber whenever in Argyll."

"Aye," Ross agreed. "He always made certain to arrive at Tòrrelise for at least one meal each day."

"And found his way to my home at Dunthoradelle for the others," Thorburn added.

"Ye sound like the dog that always knows when to find the banquet hall." She arched a brow, but the sparkle had finally returned to her eyes and for that, his brothers could say anything about him they wished.

"Did ye tell her of yer title?" Ross asked as they meandered through the gatehouse tunnel and entered the courtyard.

"For the life of me, I couldna remember it. I told her I had one. It was Baron or something of the like." Valan honestly couldn't recall because it mattered naught to him. He valued the land, and now that he was about to take a wife, he valued the tattered keep at its center. He shrugged at Elspet. "I dinna ken for certain, but I do have one."

"He has more than one title, m'lady," Thorburn said with a sidling look at his brother. "But most are nay fit for a lady's ears."

Valan hugged her closer and kissed her cheek. "Dinna change yer mind about being my wife because of my brothers. I beg ye."

Elspet laughed as they made their way to the forestair and climbed the steps. "I pray our keep will be close to theirs. I look forward to enjoying the warmth and caring of yer family." Her smile faded as she reached the landing where she always addressed the clan. At sight of the *Gallóglaigh* surrounding the castle, the alarm horns had sounded, and those of the clan who were not imprisoned, the ones who had turned a blind eye and remained silent to all the atrocities, gathered round like rats afraid they were about to be clubbed.

Valan glared at the heartless folk. The ones too young, fragile, or elderly to fight against the treason, he understood and forgave. But the others—the able-bodied men and women who could've banded together and made a difference—they deserved nothing but grief and suffering all the rest of their days.

Elspet rested both hands atop the railing and slowly scanned the gathering crowd. Then she resettled her footing as though about to do battle.

Valan moved closer and rested his hand atop hers, offering his strength.

Ross and Thorburn remained on the steps below, unsmiling and blocking the way so no one else could pass.

"In three days' time," Elspet said, her voice ringing across the courtyard, "Lady Beitris and I leave Caerlaverock. Never to return."

A low rumbling swept through the people as they turned to each other, then stole nervous glances back at Elspet. A young woman at the front stepped forward. "What about us?"

"What about ye?" Elspet said, fixing a stoic glare upon the lass.

"Who will see that we're safe? See the village rebuilt? Tend to the keep and the clan?"

Elspet shrugged, making Valan prouder with each passing moment. "None of that is my concern nor my responsibility any longer. Nor is it the responsibility of Lady Beitris."

"But ye are the lady of the keep," a man deeper in the crowd called out. "Laird Herbert said ye would always be here for us when he was called to fight. Ye always looked after Caerlaverock."

The courtyard hummed with their loud murmuring again.

"Ye say that now, yet when I was beaten and caged, when my daughter was publicly ravaged, ye said naught a word nor stepped forward to help either of us." Elspet resettled her footing again and wet her lips.

Valan squeezed her hand, ready to catch her should she swoon.

She thanked him with a grateful smile and nodded. Then she turned back and faced the crowd. "Do what ye will. I care not and willna be here to either bless yer actions or curse them. Those imprisoned will be sent to the king to hang for treason. The rest of ye can burn in Hell when ye are judged for yer lack of action to help yer kin."

Silence fell across Caerlaverock. Elspet turned and climbed the remaining steps to her floor. Valan followed close behind as did Thorburn and Ross. As soon as they entered and the door closed behind them, Elspet crumpled to the floor and covered her face with her hands.

Valan shot his brothers a look, then knelt beside her. "M'lady, my dearest heart, stand tall, my queen. I admire yer strength, yer courage, and yer dedication to all that is right."

"But I worry about the weak ones. Those who couldna help us even if they had wished to." She drew a shaking breath, rested her head on his shoulder, and closed her eyes. "What will happen to them if the others fail to thrive?"

"We shall make a list." Valan gently rocked as he hugged her. "Name the ones ye feel are innocent." He tipped her face up to his and looked down into her eyes. "We shall take the innocents to Creagshead. If they wish to come with us."

Her golden eyes widened. Relief glimmered in their depths. "Truly? Ye would do that for them?"

"I do it for you, m'lady. No one else." He might be a warrior, a fearsome *Gallóglaigh*, but he was not without a heart or conscience. "I trust Fiona and Beitris will help ye select those deserving of this choice?"

Her joyous smile filled him with the knowledge that he'd done right by his lady love. "I feel certain they will help me," she softly said. Her gaze searching his face, she rested a loving touch to his cheek. "I dinna ken what brought ye here to me, nor do I care. All I know for certain is that I love ye heart and soul, through this life, and every life thereafter."

"Ye are mine," he answered, his voice falling to a whisper. "Mine forevermore. To honor. To cherish. To love with everything I am and will ever be." After a fleeting taste of her delectable mouth, he whispered against the fullness of her lips, "I love ye, my own. For all time."

"I love ye more," she said, then pulled him down to seal the oath with a much more satisfying kiss.

EPILOGUE

Creagshead Keep
Argyll, Scotland
3 years later...

"WHERE HAS MAMA gone?" Valan danced around the back garden with his wailing daughter, making every noise and twisted face that had ever amused her. Nothing worked. His precious wee bairn was having none of it. Face red, her little bottom lip stuck out and quivering, her squalling continued without a tear in her eye. He craned his neck and peered over the stone fence surrounding the private area set off from the main courtyard.

"Elspet!" His bellow startled the unhappy toddler, making her keen even louder. "God's beard. What's wrong with Da's precious lass? Ye just ate. Mama said so. Did she nay feed ye enough?"

Instead of his wife, whom his daughter sorely needed, Thorburn and Ross pushed through the gate. Their children accompanied them, pouring in around their legs and scampering to climb on the benches and low-hanging limbs of the grand oak shading the corner.

"What have ye done to her?" Thorburn held out both hands. "Come to uncle, my precious wee lambling. Tell me all about it. What did Da refuse ye?"

"Oh, she will tell ye all right." Valan stepped to the gate and scanned the cobblestone courtyard. Servants. The smithy. The stable boy. He spotted everyone but Elspet or one of his brothers' wives.

"There's naught a tear in yer eye." Thorburn chuckled, then wrinkled his nose. With a pinched look, he turned to Valan. "Have ye lost yer sense of smell, man?"

Ross leaned closer to the child and sniffed. "God's beard. That's yer problem." He stepped back, looked up at the bank of windows overlooking the garden and yelled, "Women! A child is in need here!"

Thorburn held the lassie at arm's length as he hurried her over to her father. "Here. Ye can have her back now."

"Dinna hold her like that." Valan snatched her close, then coughed. The stench surrounding his currently not-so-sweet bairn burned his eyes. "What has yer mother been feeding ye?"

The door to the keep swung open and all three of their wives, each of them in various stages of pregnancy, entered the garden, laughing and talking.

Valan didn't wait for Elspet to reach him. Instead, he rushed over, holding the soiled child the same way he had just told Thorburn not to hold her. "Yer daughter needs ye," he said. "Badly."

Before Elspet could take her, Fiona pushed between them. "Dinna hold my Lady Rhianna like that." She took the tot and toddled away, shushing, and clucking with every hitching step. "Come, my wee lamb. Mistress Fiona will make it all better. Das canna handle such things like old Fiona."

"I hope that woman lives forever," Valan said as he watched the elderly maid disappear into the keep with his child.

"As do I, dear husband." Elspet eyed him with a sly grin. "Serves ye right though, bragging ye could tend to yer daughter with no trouble at all."

"I can." He hugged her to his side. "When she's clean, dry, and fed, she and I have a grand time playing here in the garden."

Either Thorburn or Ross snickered. He didn't know which

until Adellis swatted Thorburn's arm. "Dinna be laughing at yer brother. Ye're the same with Mathan and Ian, and I am sure ye will be the same with this one when it comes." She patted her rounded belly.

"If we dinna feed the rest of the bairns, Rhianna will nay be the only one greetin'." Elspet waved them all toward the table and benches laid out beside the herb gardens. "Cook's prepared a fine feast for us to enjoy on this fine sunny day."

Adellis and Elise clapped their hands. The young ones came running and climbed onto the benches. Thorburn and Ross settled in their midst, ensuring everyone's plates were filled.

Valan stood aside, his arm still around Elspet, taking in the scene. He could stand like this forever, soaking in the contentment of family.

"Are ye not hungry?" Elspet gently patted his chest as she leaned against him.

"Nay, m'love. I am hungry for nothing. I have everything I need right here."

She smiled up at him and snuggled closer. "As do I, m'love. As do I."

About the Author

If you enjoyed A SCOT TO LOVE AND PROTECT, please consider leaving a review on the site where you purchased your copy, or a reader site such as Goodreads, or BookBub.

If you'd like to receive my newsletter, here's the link to sign up:
maevegreyson.com/contact.html#newsletter

I love to hear from readers! Drop me a line at:
maevegreyson@gmail.com

Or visit me on Facebook:
facebook.com/AuthorMaeveGreyson

Join my Facebook Group – Maeve's Corner:
facebook.com/groups/MaevesCorner

I'm also on Instagram:
maevegreyson

My website:
https://maevegreyson.com

Feel free to ask questions or leave some Reader Buzz on:
bingebooks.com/author/maeve-greyson

Follow me on these sites to get notifications about new releases, sales, and special deals:
Amazon:
amazon.com/Maeve-Greyson/e/B004PE9T9U

BookBub:
bookbub.com/authors/maeve-greyson

Many thanks, and may your life always be filled with good books!
Maeve

CPSIA information can be obtained
at www.ICGtesting.com
Printed in the USA
LVHW040345140123
737053LV00014B/1266

9 781958 098493